Winter Vendetta

Winter Vendetta

TERRELL L. BOWERS

Br. Collec.
ω

AVALON BOOKS
THOMAS BOUREGY AND COMPANY, INC.
401 LAFAYETTE STREET
NEW YORK, NEW YORK 10003

PRINTED IN THE UNITED STATES OF AMERICA
ON ACID-FREE PAPER
BY HADDON CRAFTSMEN, SCRANTON, PENNSYLVANIA

Winter Vendetta

Chapter One

Dave Bryant jerked his horse to a stop on the high mountain ridge. Then he strained his ears against the usual sounds of the forest and the mountain creatures. The shriek could have been that of a hawk, or of a distant animal.

The scream pierced the air a second time, a frantic cry of unholy terror. Putting his heels to his mount, Dave plunged into the dense thicket of wild currant. There was no doubt that the cries were of human origin. Somewhere below, hidden by the trees, practically drowned out by the roar of a nearby waterfall, a woman was in desperate trouble.

Reining his horse through the trees, he went down the hill in bounds. He searched the area below, able to see the stream of water in one clearing. The shadow that flashed through the brush wore something white and flowing that was catching on the sharp edges of branches and thorns. He got only a glimpse, but he could see it was a woman.

"Here!" he called, guiding his horse in a direction to intercept her. "Over here!"

The crack of a gun broke his horse's stride. Its legs buckled under him and he went down. Dave kicked his feet loose from the stirrups and went over the horse's head. He landed in a leafy shrub that helped to break his fall.

A second blast took his hat off, and he scrambled behind a fallen log, clawing out his own gun. He searched the hillside, his eyes darting about frantically, trying to spot the gunman.

Someone came crashing through the brush behind him, and he spun to meet him, gun aligned, finger on the trigger.

The girl, who had already run past him, stopped so fast that she fell to her knees. She pulled up the torn white dress to cover herself as she crawled back toward Dave. She pointed toward the stream.

"He's there!" she gasped. "By the water!"

Dave swung his attention back to the creek. He had his gun ready and searched with his eyes, trying to find a target. The girl rose to her hands and knees, and carefully peeked over the wall of foliage. He couldn't listen for the gunman because she was breathing heavily, exhausted by her hasty escape.

"Just one man?" he asked, seeing no movement.

"Yes," she gasped. "It's him! It's the Butcher!"

Dave had no idea what she meant, but he had a score to settle with the skunk who had killed his horse and ventilated his hat. There could be no doubt that the man was dangerous.

As they crouched there together, Dave heard a horse beating a path through the trees.

"He's on the run!" Dave cried, but as he came to his feet and was about to run through the trees and attempt to cut him off, the girl caught hold of his arm.

"No! Don't!" She was wide-eyed, still suffering from the terrifying experience. "If you leave me, he . . . he might. . . ."

With a sigh of defeat, Dave holstered his gun. Anyway, the gunman was on horseback and would have been hard to catch on foot.

"He would have killed me," the girl said shakily. "I was down swimming when he came out of no-where. He had his knife out. I barely got across the stream ahead of him. If you hadn't arrived when you did. . . ."

Dave saw the girl shiver. It could have been from the early-fall air, but he guessed it was more from the realization that she had nearly been killed. She appeared to be in her late teens or very early twenties, but there was a maturity in her voice that seemed advanced for her age. Frightened as she was, she demonstrated a remarkable composure. She held her torn dress together. There were a number of scratches on her legs from running through the brush. Her feet were even worse, for the ground was littered with sticks and sharp rocks.

Dave told her, "Do what you can with your clothes. I've got some medicine in my saddlebag for your feet and legs. Wouldn't do to get an infection."

Then she noticed his horse, still lying where it had fallen, killed by the unknown assailant's first bullet.

"I'm sorry about your horse," she said quietly.

"Me too," Dave replied, moving over to remove the disinfectant from the pack. "He was a game steed."

The girl was calm by the time he returned with some bandages and ointment. She was sitting on a rotted log, examining a nasty cut on the side of her foot. She had raven-black hair like that of an Indian or Mexican, but her blue-gray eyes gave evidence of her white descent. She had a petite face, oval, with inviting lips and a delicate nose. The whiteness about her shoulders had been evident before, but was now adequately covered by the torn, ragged dress. Still, he knew that her skin was as white and soft-looking as a cotton ball. As he looked at her, she pulled back the hair that draped onto her shoulders. The action displayed a womanly posture that kindled a spark of interest within him.

Making an effort to remain objective, Dave knelt down at her feet and brushed the dirt from the bruises and cuts. He cleaned them with antiseptic, and then bandaged one entire foot and the sole and heel of the other. She held her dress up to her knees so that he was able to tend to scratches above her ankles. He was hard-pressed to ignore the shapeliness of her legs.

"You have a very gentle touch for a man."

He suspected that she spoke to cover the embarrassment of having a strange man treat her injuries.

"You wouldn't be a doctor or something?" she went on.

He grinned inwardly. His hands were soft, but it was because of his trade. Except for his rawhide-tough knuckles from boxing, he seldom did any physical labor.

"Up until a few weeks back, I was a traveling sales representative."

Her brows lifted. "Really? What kind of salesman were you—a drummer of dry goods or pots and pans?"

His grin surfaced. "No, ma'am. I used to sell for the Remington Arms Company."

"Oh," she said. "Guns."

He chuckled at the usual response. "No. Type-writers."

"But I thought the Remington Arms Company made guns."

"That's true enough, but they also sell typewriters. You'd be surprised to know that the newer models have a shift key for making either small or capital letters."

"What a big improvement! I saw a typing machine in Billings once, but it printed only in capitals and smeared ink all over the paper."

"Progress," he said simply.

"We met rather abruptly. I'm Colette Striker," she introduced herself cordially.

Dave stopped dabbing the ointment on a scratch below her knee and rocked back on his heels. The shock must have shown plainly on his face.

"Striker!" he repeated the hated name. "You're not related to Henry Striker?"

A frown darkened her face. "By my mother's second marriage. He's my stepfather."

Dave tried to hide the rage that swelled in his chest. *I come three hundred miles to kill Henry Striker, and the first thing that happens is that I save the man's daughter from some unknown killer.*

"Do you know Henry?" Colette's voice was hesitant. She had witnessed his strong reaction and seemed uncertain of how to proceed.

"I . . . I know of him and his sons," he evaded carefully. "I never knew about any second marriage."

"During the uprising of '75, the Sioux burned our home to the ground and killed my father. Mother had no family and had been courted by Henry in her youth. We bounced around for a couple of hard, lean years. Then Mother ran into Henry and he invited us to stay with him. We really had no place else to go. Mother married him a year after we joined him at the ranch."

Dave regained a firm control on his emotions. "And what about you? What do you think of Henry and his sons?"

Colette paused before speaking. "Henry treats me all right, but he lets Jake and Tom run the place. The boys enjoy giving me a rough time sometimes, and it seems that I work sixteen hours a day, but I have little choice in the matter. I can't leave until I either marry or reach the age of twenty-one."

He wondered how long that wait would be, but did not ask. "Maybe Jake or Tommy will want you for a wife."

"No chance of that," she said with relief. "That's one reason my mother had my name changed to Striker—it eliminated any chance of a marriage."

Dave thought that a bit odd, considering that the woman had married a Striker herself. Maybe the woman was one of those lost, drowning souls, unable to cope in the sea of life. Henry had been the only lifeboat she had managed to find. He had certainly never struck Dave as a woman's man. Jake and Tom's mother had been mean-tempered and as homely as a lop-eared mule. She had likely married Henry because he was the only one able to put up with her.

"You haven't told me your name," the girl interrupted his thoughts. "Who do I owe my life to?"

Dave couldn't tell her his last name, for the Strikers would undoubtedly remember the Bryants. And it would be foolish to use a common alias like Smith or Jones. The only name that popped into his head was the town where he had lived for the past five years—Valley Run, Wyoming.

"It's Dave, Dave Valeron," he answered.

The girl smiled, her already pretty face lighting up with a luminous glow.

"Well, Mr. Valeron, I have a horse across the stream. I doubt that he can carry your saddle and belongings, but if you'll see me home, I'll ask Henry to lend you another mount. It's small payment for my life."

Dave took a moment to stare in the direction the bushwhacker had taken in his escape.

"Who would try to kill you?"

Colette appeared to suffer from a chill once more. "He wore a black hood over his face." She shivered and wrapped her arms around herself. "No one knows who the Butcher is, but three girls have died in the past eight months. I'm sure he was the one responsible."

"He attacks only girls?"

"They've all been unmarried girls between sixteen and twenty years old. He killed one with an ax and the other two were stabbed to death. They were horribly murdered, Mr. Valeron. The killer is called the Butcher, a fitting name for such a crazed madman."

"I wish I'd gotten a decent shot at him. I hate the thought of a creature like that running around loose."

"Every girl in the valley is living in fear for her life. They don't go out after dark, and it's even dangerous to be out during daylight hours alone. I never dreamed that he would be out here in the woods."

"You had a close call all right. Good thing you're fast on your feet."

Colette looked down at her torn dress. "Henry is going to be awfully angry at me. This is the only good dress I own, and I was supposed to come straight home after the church meeting."

"Why didn't you?"

She ducked her head, obviously embarrassed. "I wanted to bathe. Tom and Jake make it very difficult for me to have any privacy at the ranch. I practically have to sleep in my clothes to avoid their spying."

It was exactly the way Dave remembered them, a real pair of coyotes. He had never had a fight with just one. Always it had been the two of them ganging up on him. Even after ten long years, he remembered the beatings they had given him.

"I'll get your horse," he said. Then he saw the fear shining in her eyes.

"Can I go with you? I don't wish to be alone just yet."

Without wasting words, Dave turned about, slipped his arm under her legs, and lifted her from the log.

"I didn't mean for you to carry me," she protested.

"I just spent ten minutes bandaging your feet. You aren't going to ruin my handiwork by walking."

She didn't reply to that and slipped her arm about his neck. It was disquieting, feeling the girl against him, smelling the shampoo in her hair, having her damp body in his arms. He had not had much time for female companionship in the past, even though he had met a number of women through his selling. He had worked toward only one goal, returning to Scofield, Montana.

Dave reached the water's edge and waded the stream carefully. Colette directed him to her horse and he set her up in the saddle. After gathering her shoes and stockings, he tucked them into his shirt for easy transport. Then he swung up behind her and started the animal toward the Striker ranch.

"What brings you to our part of the country, Mr.

Valeron?'' Colette asked when they were clear of the trees.

It sounded strange to be called by such a name, and Dave already felt the pangs of guilt for lying. For the time being, he had to keep his identity a secret. The truth would come out soon enough, but it had to wait for the right occasion. He could not very well tell her that he had come to kill her step-father and brothers, and so it meant telling a second lie:

''I'm looking to do some business in the area. I figured to rest my horse in Scofield, but he won't need it now.''

''I'm sorry about the loss of your horse.''

''Better him than you, ma'am,'' he said, enjoying the way she seemed to lean back against him.

They crossed a range of rolling hills and then dropped into a meadow from where Dave could see the Lazy S spread. The Striker ranch was up one canyon, with miles of grazing land to the east. Up the other direction, the Box Z stretched endless miles toward Idaho. He well remembered the layout of the two places, for his family had owned the small ranch that lay between them. There had been no reason to force them out, to kill his mother and father, but that is what Striker had done.

Twelve years had passed since that nightmarish event. Dave had been in his mid-teens. If not for Pecos Thorn getting him out of the valley, he would probably have been killed as well. The fires of anger still burned brightly, and Dave's teeth clenched in hatred. Twelve long years in hiding, learning the art of self-defense, shooting, handling a knife, boxing. He had learned these skills well, and they were dedicated to a single cause—revenge!

Chapter Two

The Striker place was the way he remembered it from occasional visits with his folks. The sprawling ranch house still had weeds growing out of its sod roof, and the porch sported two chairs under the protection of the eaves. The shuttered windows were open to either side of the single door near the middle of the house. It was gray and chipped with age, still in need of paint or stain that it had never received. The corrals were next to the barn and tack shed, with a bunkhouse to either side of the rear of the house. As they entered the yard, a homely brute stepped out into the sun. Even though it had been twelve years, Dave recognized the big brother of the family, Jake Striker.

"Where 'n the devil you been, Sparrow!" Jake

snarled at Colette. "Pa is gonna round up the horse-whip!"

"I haven't done anything wrong," she replied meekly.

Jake stood indolently, hands on his hips, jaw thrust forward. His eyes raked over Colette and then stopped, riveted to Dave.

"Pa!" he called out over his shoulder. "You'd best come out here and have a look at this."

Dave reined the horse over next to the house. He dismounted opposite the Striker boy quickly, before he could come around the horse. By that time, he was able to get Colette down from the saddle, and he took her into his arms and carried her past the gaping Jake to the porch. He set her down carefully and then pulled her shoes and socks from inside his shirt. The old man tramped onto the porch as he was handing them to Colette.

"Well, now." Henry's voice sounded like a rusty gate's swing. "What's been going on, gal? Who's this fella, and what's he doing, carrying your shoes around in his shirt?"

Careful to keep his back to the wall of the building, Dave met the man face-to-face. There was no change after twelve years. Henry was still arrogant and demanding, with his piggish eyes still shining like two coals reflecting the sun's glare. And he still looked tough enough to chew barbed wire. He was at least six feet tall and about two hundred pounds.

Jake stepped up to his side, shadowing him by a couple of inches and twenty pounds. They both dwarfed Dave's five-ten and a hundred and seventy pounds.

"I—I went to bathe after church, Mr. Striker," Colette attempted to explain. "That man who's been killing girls almost caught me. He would have too, but Mr. Valeron here heard my screams and managed to run the Butcher off."

Henry's face expressed indifference. "So the killer was after you and you cut up your feet running away?"

"I didn't have time to do anything else," she went on quickly. "One minute I was alone, and the next I was running for my life."

The tough owner of the Lazy S stepped over in front of the girl. He looked her up and down, then took hold of a piece of torn material. He shook his head, his face red with anger.

"Blast your foolish and selfish hide!" he snarled. "You were supposed to come straight home! I give you a little slack and you try and romp wild and free. Look what you done to your Sunday best!"

The girl cringed from his wrath. Henry's voice was still bold and authoritative, and he used it like a club, knocking her down with the sheer force of his words.

"Ought to take the horsewhip to her, Pa," Jake sneered. "Seems that Sparrow is more like a bird all the time, fluttering about and flying from here to who knows where. She don't never mind you no more. If you ain't got the stomach for a good whipping, I sure have!''

Dave's temper flared, but he held it in check. His hand firmly grasped the butt of his gun. How he ached to draw down on the skunks in front of him.

Don't do it! he told himself firmly. *You'll have your revenge, all of it. Don't rush their end. It would be doing them a favor.*

The old man spun on Dave with fire in his eyes and with suspicion twisting his features.

''And what've you got to say about this whole thing, mister? Where's your horse?''

''The man who intended to kill the young lady here had better luck with my mount. I thought you might lend me one of yours until I get my gear into town.''

''This ain't no livery stable,'' Jake growled.

''Mr. Valeron saved my life!'' Colette shouted. ''It's my fault that his horse was killed!''

Jake took a menacing step toward her. She cowered at once and raised her hands to cover her face. The action indicated that she was used to getting knocked around by him. To Dave, it was one more log on the fires of his hate.

''Jake!'' Henry yelled at his boy. Then he flicked a sour glance toward the girl. ''You hush your mouth, Colette! One more word out of you and I'll take a whip to you. You hear me, girl?''

Colette straightened and lowered her hands from the protective posture. "Please, Mr. Striker. Won't you let Mr. Valeron have the use of a horse? It isn't much repayment for my life."

"More 'n she's worth, if you ask me," Jake growled.

Dave stepped off the porch and regarded the two men with a smirk of contempt. He spat into the dirt at Henry's feet.

"You keep your stinking, coyote-bait nags, Striker. I don't want to owe you one blessed thing."

Henry narrowed his gaze. "What were you doing up there in the hills, anyway? You wouldn't have been spying on my girl?"

"That's it!" Jake jeered, stepping forward. "Bet he was trying to get a look at Colette while she was taking a bath."

"No!" Colette cried. "How can you be so stubborn blind?" She grabbed Henry by the arm and tried to turn him round. It was a mistake, for Jake reached out and clouted her with a solid backhand. Knocked backward on the porch, she landed hard on the wooden planks, her dress up above her knees.

"There you are!" Jake guffawed. "Take another look, you sneaking polecat!"

Dave had reached his limit. He doubled his fists and planted himself in front of Jake.

"You're a real tough man, Jake," he said with open contempt. "Pretty courageous of you to slap around a girl half your size. Maybe you'd care to try that with me?"

"How'd you know my name?"

"You smell like a Jake to me," Dave replied. "I knew a man who owned a pig by that name." He put on a crooked grin. "That pig had gas something awful."

Jake glowered at Dave, his huge hands balled into fists. He raised his arms and waded forward, yelling, "I'm gonna rub your nose in the dirt. I'll show you who's the tough man around here."

Dave waited, his feet set, balanced, ready. He had trained hard to learn to fight, and had developed his punching from hours of hitting sawdust-filled bags and from strenuous exercises. Endless hours of practice had given him keen reflexes and power in his blows.

Colette smoothed her skirt down to her ankles. Then she dabbed at a trickle of blood that ran from her lip. The revulsion that Dave had carried and nurtured over the years was multiplied from the sight. He harnessed his hatred and remained poised, letting the brute come to him.

Jake was powerfully built, with broad shoulders, a thick chest, and massive arms. He squinted past his broad Roman nose, put on a sneer that twisted his thick lips, and waded in like an enraged bear.

Dave ducked a wild right hand, blocked a short left, then exploded his right fist against Jake's nose. Before Jake could even utter a howl of pain, Dave smashed his lips against the yellow-stained teeth.

Jake backstepped, trying to get his guard up. As he lifted his hands, Dave drove a pile-driving right-left combination to his solar plexus. It brought a surprised grunt from Jake.

Ducking from a flurry of punches, Dave kept his distance, watched for an opening, and then struck again. He devastated Jake's nose with a right cross that broke bone. Then he bashed the big man's lips with a wicked left. Jake was staggering, but Dave gave him no quarter. He punished him, slamming him full in the face, cracking his ribs with the tremendous power of his blows. It was not until Jake went down into the dirt that Dave stopped his assault. He was not surprised to find two guns pointing at him when he stepped away from the beaten man.

Tom Striker was not so big as his brother, but he was every bit as ugly. He held a shotgun between his hands and a black scowl creased his face. Henry had pulled a Navy Colt and was pointing it at Dave's head.

"Jake has had enough," Henry said. "You'd best get off our place while both of your legs still work."

Dave lowered his guard, satisfied that he had given Jake a sound beating. He had not been touched during the short brawl. His training had paid off.

"If you Strikers are quite through thanking me for saving the young lady's life, I'll be heading for town," Dave said. "It's still ten miles and I'd like to get my things off my horse before dark."

"Why'd you come to Bear County, boy?"

Dave grinned indolently at Henry. "That's *my* business. You'll find out in good time. Meanwhile, don't you worry about it none."

"You'd better worry that I don't pull the trigger on this here shotgun!" Tom warned.

Dave put a hard look on him. "When you're threatening a man, you'd best have those hammers pulled back. I could kill you twice before you ever got off a shot."

"Maybe *I* wouldn't be so slow to fire," Henry put in. "Just 'cause I preach on Sundays don't mean I can't kill me a snake."

That put a crooked grin on Dave's face. "You do the sermonizing on Sundays?" He laughed at the thought. "Talk about Lucifer telling the saints how to behave."

"Get off our place, Valeron!" Henry roared. "Get off while you can still walk!"

Dave tipped his hat to a very bewildered Colette, and then he turned and started walking. It was a long walk but he had a spring of energy in his step. His knuckles were scarred and bleeding a little, but he felt good, real good.

* * *

Colette ran her tongue along the cut inside her lip. The salty taste of blood still lingered, and there was a small lump where the skin had made contact with her teeth. When the door to her room opened, she grabbed her dress to cover herself.

As it turned out, the act was not necessary, for it was Sela, her mother. There was worry etched on her face. She held a wad of cloth and a bottle of medicine in her hand.

"You look like you ran through a briar patch in your birthday suit, dear. You must have a dozen scratches on each leg."

Colette lifted the dress she had removed minutes before. "I didn't do any good to my dress, either. I'm afraid that it's ruined."

Sela came forward and took the dress from her. She dropped it into a heap and shook her head.

"I'll see what I can find to replace it. I know that Sunday is the only day Henry lets you have any time for yourself."

Colette sat down on the edge of her bed, allowing her mother to examine her feet and scratches.

"Jake looks a sight," Sela said softly, as if afraid that someone in the family would overhear her words. "That man certainly gave him a pounding. His nose is busted, his ribs are cracked, and he lost three teeth. It's for certain that he won't be eating any steak for a spell."

"He asked for it," Colette said firmly. "I know

it isn't Christian, but it did my heart good to see him finally get his due. He's been making my life miserable for years.''

Sela nodded in sympathy. ''I know, dear, and I'm sorry there's nothing I can do. Henry lets Jake do whatever he pleases. He can't seem to put his foot down where that boy is concerned.''

''He's nearly thirty and still thinks like a nasty brat. I used to pray he'd have an accident and be crippled, so he could no longer torment me.'' Colette sighed. ''I guess God doesn't solve our problems that way.''

''Henry doesn't believe in sparing the rod and spoiling the child, dear. It's some consolation that he doesn't punish you himself.''

''He couldn't be worse than Jake. I'm no child anymore, Mother. I'm almost twenty. When do I get any rights to speak or act as I please around here?''

''Henry has always felt that a woman's place was behind her man, with her mouth shut. He treats me decent, but he won't take my side against his precious boys.''

''I still can't believe they'd be so ungrateful. The man saved my life, Mother, and they insinuated that he was trying to watch me bathe.''

''Perhaps they think all men think and behave the way they do. How did the man happen to save you?''

''He was traveling on the mountain trail above

the stream. He heard my cries for help and came to my rescue. Until he heard me scream, he didn't know that anyone else was around.''

"Thank God he did hear you.''

"Henry could sure use a little of the religion he preaches,'' Colette said. "He didn't thank him and he accused him of spying. Mr. Valeron's horse was killed by the Butcher, and he ends up walking clear to town. You chose a real knight in shining armor for a husband, Mother.''

Sela's shoulders sagged under the weight of her words. "I'm sorry, dear. I had no idea that your life would be so miserable here. Henry was once a much different man. When he offered to take us in, I was desperate. We had no money, no food, no home. It seemed the answer to our prayers.''

"But you don't love him.''

Sela studied her feet as she shuffled uneasily under Colette's accusation.

"Love is a nice word, but necessity is more realistic. I married Henry for the security he offered the two of us. If it weren't for Tom and Jake being such bullies, he wouldn't be hard to live with.''

"I hate all three of them,'' Colette said. "I can't help it—that's the way I feel.''

Sela appeared shocked that she would say such a thing outright. Colette had held her tongue and put up with abuse for over seven years, and it came as a surprise that she would suddenly show a fighting spirit.

''Did you get a look at the attacker?'' she hurriedly changed the train of the conversation.

''No. He wore a hood that covered his entire head. I was on the shore, dressed except for my shoes and stockings. He came out of nowhere with a terrible knife raised over his head as if he was going to split me like a chicken. I splashed back into the water and beat him across the stream. The dress caught on the tree branches and brush, but I ran screaming at the top of my lungs.''

''That's when this other man rode up?''

''He came charging down the hill on his horse, but the Butcher shot the animal out from under him. I managed to get safely to his side, and the killer broke and ran.''

''And you said his name was what?''

''Dave Valeron.''

Sela regarded Colette closely. ''He must have made quite an impression on you. First the rescue from the Butcher, then he takes up for you and knocks Jake flatter than a watered-down flapjack.''

Colette recognized the insinuating look in her mother's eyes. But instead of being ashamed, she demonstrated her defiance and said, ''He acted like a man, Mother. I don't know any other way to put it. He was willing to take on the Butcher in a fight to the death, and he defended both his own honor and mine against Jake.'' She allowed herself a whisper of a smile. "Amazing, the power in those fists of his. I thought that he had extremely gentle hands for a man. He said that he sold typewriters for a living.''

Sela raised her brows. "Jake was whipped by a typewriter salesman?'' She even gave a very rare laugh. "Wait till Jake hears about that. It'll hurt him more than the beating.''

Colette laughed along with her mother. It was a rare moment between them. In fact, she could not recall the last time they had laughed together.

"Best get dressed now, dear,'' Sela said, the moment lost. "Supper is going to be late. We don't want Henry having reason to be more angry about the events of this afternoon.''

Colette donned her cotton work dress and then gingerly slipped on her shoes. She was still in pain from the cuts on her feet, but there was work to be done. Her hair was in total disarray from being wet and not having been combed out, but the men on the ranch were more concerned with how the food tasted than how well groomed the cook was. With a fleeting image of Dave Valeron still lingering in her mind's eye, she left the sanctity of her room. As usual, there was no time for rest or daydreaming.

Chapter Three

S cofield was not a big town. There were only two big ranches, a few small farms, and the small but steady stream of travelers who used the northern route toward Canada to support business. It did, however, have a courthouse. There was a judge who not only served the legal affairs of the community but who was also the clerk and recorder for the land office, keeping track of records and deeds of title.

Because it was a Sunday, Dave entered town to find most of the streets deserted. He walked down the main thoroughfare, recalling the stores and buildings he had grown used to as a child. The Red Moose Saloon was still the main building, with an upstairs that often served as a hotel. The general store appeared to have changed ownership, for Dave did not recognize the name on the front. The jail was a new addition, sitting directly across from the courthouse, but the dress shop, the tinsmith, the barber's and the leather-goods and saddlery shops were all as he remembered them.

A few feet from the livery stable he was confronted by a big man with a badge. Even as a young man Ed Rutledge had been called Big Ed. He had not changed all that much except his chest seemed to have slipped. It now sagged into his basement, spilling over his belt at the middle. Dave remembered him as being stoutly built, but he had grown paunchy with the years.

"Don't see many gamblers on foot," Ed said pointedly. "Did you miss the stage?"

"You've got me wrong, Sheriff. I gamble for fun, but I'm a salesman by trade."

"With that black suit and fancy, silver-banded Stetson, I guessed you to be a cardsharp."

Dave offered a smile of truce. "A salesman ought to look good for his business contacts."

Ed tipped his head toward the end of town. His shrewd eyes were shaded by a white skimmer hat. "What you doing on foot? I seen you a-coming a long way off."

"My horse was shot out from under me a few miles back in the hills. I need to rent another one, so I can return and get my tack and gear."

That sparked Ed's attention at once. "Someone shot your horse?"

"Some jasper was trying to kill Colette Striker. She thought it was the character known as the Butcher."

Ed lifted his brows at the news. "No kidding? The Butcher made a try at Colette?"

"I didn't get a look at him. He gunned down my horse, and when I heard the lady screaming, I came to her aid. He ran off before I could get a look or shot at him."

"How about Colette? Is she all right? Did *she* get a look at him?"

"She said he wore a mask, a hood that covered his head. He didn't get his hands on her. You want to ride back with me and take a look around?"

Big Ed grunted. "That guy don't leave any clues. Three murders so far and we know absolutely nothing about him. For no apparent reason, he up and kills some poor creature every few weeks. I ain't been sleeping nights, worrying about where he'll strike next."

"Can you help me rent a horse on a Sunday?"

"Just bang on the livery gate. Dinky is around someplace."

"Thanks."

Ed looked closely at Dave. "You look vaguely familiar. Do I know you from somewhere?"

"Could be. I get around."

Ed scratched his chin, and then narrowed his eyes in thought. "There's something about you, but I can't recollect from where or when."

"It'll come to you, Ed."

"You know my name?"

"Heard it mentioned up at the Striker place. I was going to get the loan of a horse from Henry, but that didn't pan out."

"I'd think Henry would have given you the shirt off his back. He sure preaches that sort of thing on Sunday mornings."

"Jake kind of got mixed up into our conversation. After our discussion, Henry wasn't feeling real sociable."

Ed's eyes roamed over him, and they came to rest on a red stain on his shirt. "That looks like blood on your clothes. You say the Butcher didn't hurt Colette?"

"She was scratched up from running through the brush, but. . . ." Dave grinned. "The blood is Jake Striker's. I told you that we exchanged words."

"Looks like it was more than words," Ed said with a glint of respect in his eyes. "You took Jake in a fair fight?"

"A traveling drummer has to be able to defend himself. I took a little air out of Jake's sails, but he'll be up and bullying again in no time."

"Jake's a bully all right. But I've not seen anyone call his bluff before now."

"He said and did a couple of things that I won't put up with—from anyone."

Ed noticed the battered knuckles on Dave's hands. A smile spread across his lips. He was a homely brute, with big hands and feet, and a face long enough for a horse, and he was built like an upside-down tepee. Other than that, he had been fair-minded in his younger days. That he disliked Jake openly was also in his favor.

"I'm thinking you might be more than meets the eye," he told Dave. "You ain't got a mark on you except for your knuckles."

"I discovered at a young age that it was less painful to hit someone than to be hit by him."

"So what's your handle, salesman?"

"Dave Valeron."

Ed extended his hand. "I'm proud to meet the man who dimmed Jake's lamps for him. I've considered doing it myself a few times, but never got around to it."

Dave took the hand in a short, firm shake. "He was begging to be taken down a notch or two."

"That's his style," Ed agreed.

"What about the Butcher?"

Ed rubbed his chin. "I'd like to have a look around, but I hurt my back a couple of days ago, and I can't sit a horse without suffering. I'd appreciate your looking around for me. If there are any clues at all, I'll take a buggy and ride out there."

"I'm no professional tracker, but I'll sure check for sign."

They parted company then, with Ed lumbering up the street toward the other end of town. He didn't walk as if he were suffering from a stiff back, but there was no reason to doubt his claim.

Dave walked toward the livery. It was growing late, and he would be lucky to get out to his dead horse before sundown. That would not leave much time for a thorough search.

The man sat his horse in the shadow of the tall pines, his eyes still burning like the dying embers of a night fire. The turmoil and rage tore him apart. Anger, hate, and blood lust all churned within his chest. He removed his knife from its sheath and studied the razor-sharp blade in the late-afternoon dusk.

"I had her," he said, his teeth clenched tightly. "She would have been mine!" He cursed under his breath, confounded by the bad luck that had allowed Colette to escape him. The humility burned white-hot, searing his senses, fanning his uncontrollable hatred. He shut his eyes in pain while he viewed the girl's image in his mind.

Colette had been swimming like a child, clad only in her dainty chemise, which was white and inno-cent, the same as she. Her body had been glistening and magnificent, tantalizing him, hypnotizing him.

He had waited, not breaking the serenity of her bath, actually enjoying the tune she sang. She had been a delightful water nymph and ripe for sacrifice. If only he had gotten a good hold on her. . . .

The man's head snapped up, and his eyes searched the terrain below. How long had he sat there? An hour? Two hours? He shook his head in confusion. The day was nearly gone. Had he ridden to town and returned? Had he gone home and come back to this spot? Or had he spent all afternoon pining the loss of his prey? He didn't know.

Far below, weaving through the trees, a rider in black appeared. It was the man who had interrupted his encounter with Colette!

He watched as the man rode over to his dead horse, and then he reined his own mount deeper into the shadows. He was a fool to still be in the area. What if a posse boiled out of town in search of him? He might have bluffed his way through it, but his presence would have aroused suspicions. He could not let anyone stop him from his goals.

For a moment, the man far below looked up the hill—directly at him. He knew the man couldn't possibly know he was there, but a few men possessed a sixth sense and knew when someone was watching them. The man in black might possess such a warning device in his makeup and he would be a challenge if the two of them should ever meet in combat.

After a while, the man below began to unsaddle

his fallen horse. Then, like a fleeting shadow, the Butcher eased his way through the trees and picked up the main trail. The tracks of his horse would be lost in the frequent travel along the trail. He reversed direction after a short distance and stuck with the road for a time. Then he cut away, using the cover of solid rock to hide his exit. No one would be able to follow his tracks.

The Butcher swallowed his disappointment and dejection. He could not dwell on the loss, for Colette would one day be vulnerable again. He would bide his time, watch for her to sneak away for a swim or a nap, and then he would have his vengeance. She had no right to drive him to such depths of deprivation. She brutally abused his shattered mind with her sensuous curves, and the way she swayed when she walked, and the beauty of her features. She was a torment to him, and he would end that torment. She would suffer as he did, and go through the agonies of hell before she felt the wonderful relief of death.

The Butcher was lost to the deep shadows of dusk as he moved through the thick, tall pines and birch. He would also deal with the man in black one day, for he had ruined a very special moment.

"Turn not your back, my friend," he said aloud, warning Dave Valeron without knowing his name. "One night, dark and cold, I shall have my revenge on you too. I should have stayed and killed you today, but I let you live. Enjoy it while you can, for you have a gambler's luck.''

Dave paused and stared up the mountainside once more. It could have been his imagination, but he thought he could detect the distant echo of hoofbeats. He wondered if someone was coming, but the sounds were soon gone, lost in the waning of the sun's last rays of light. He tried to shake the eerie feeling that swept over him. It had to be his mind playing tricks on him, caused by the memory of nearly being killed on that very spot. The presence he felt was a cold chill, a dead cold that penetrated through his jacket and vest. It was something evil and sinister that lingered in the air, as if the Butcher still lurked in the woods.

Touching the butt of his gun for security, Dave watched his borrowed horse for any reaction. The animal was busy munching on a stand of grass, unable to detect any unsavory presence.

You're becoming afraid of ghosts, Dave warned himself. *Next thing you know, you'll be running from shadows*.

The sound of his footsteps was hollow against the still of the woods and the flowing water below. He walked the area until dusk, but there were no clues, no marks that were readable. He found nothing to point a finger at who the Butcher might be.

He hooked his saddle over the back of the horse

and dropped his saddlebags over the neck of the animal. With a final backward glance, he headed for town. He was relieved to be out of the dark forest of trees and brush. He tried to shrug off the feeling that haunted him, but it lingered for miles. By the time he saw the lights of town, he was satisfied that it had been nothing.

Dave took the horse to the stable and found a room over the saloon for the night. After a quick supper he went right to bed, exhausted from the long trek and the events of the day.

Sleep did not come, however, because his purpose still agitated his thoughts. He had come to Scofield to pay a blood debt to Henry Striker and his sons. It was not a cheerful thought, because revenge eats at a man's insides until he is void of all other feelings. It weakens his compassion toward others and feeds on his soul. Unless softened in some peaceful way, it would consume him completely. And yet he would have his vengeance, no matter what the cost. He had planned and lived for the days ahead.

Lying in the dark, staring at the ceiling, Dave reflected on his last night in the valley. It had been a night of terror to a teenage boy, for he had found his mother's lifeless body while it was still warm. She had been killed by a single blow to the head. His father was gunned down in the yard minutes later, shot and killed by Henry Striker and his two sons. If not for Pecos's grabbing him and dragging him out into the night, he might well have been killed with his parents.

Dave shut his eyes, hating the haunting memories. He tried to think of something less painful, because he needed the relief and recuperation of sleep to give him strength for another day. Amid his broken images and the blur of faces, he discovered a vision of beauty—Colette Striker. With a picture of Colette to force away the dark images, he could relax . . . and sleep.

Chapter Four

Judge Hammer pounded the table with his long, skinny finger. He was beside himself with exasperation.

"Ain't you listening to me, Valeron? You looking at where I'm pointing?"

"I can read a map," Dave replied evenly.

"This deed you've got is for the Bryant spread. It sits squarely between the Lazy S and the Box Z ranches. It controls the only water that the Lazy S has at this time of year."

"I'm aware of that, Judge," Dave said patiently, unmoved by the man's emotional outbursts.

"Then you got to know that the Strikers aren't going to let you move in and close off their water hole."

"It's not their water, Judge," Dave countered. "I've got the deed, remember? Sam and Mary Bryant purchased that piece of ground back in 1870. They owned it, before Henry Striker even showed up with his cattle. As for Axell Braggs, the owner of the Box Z, he inherited it from his uncle and doesn't need the water because of the creek flowing through his property."

"But that ain't the point, Valeron. You're fixing to start a war with the Lazy S ranch. I can't approve of that."

"I'm not asking you to approve of anything, Judge. All I'm doing is showing you a receipt for the back taxes that I paid on the Bryant place. I've got a surveyor arriving in a day or two, and he'll mark off the land with stakes. After that, I'll be putting in barbed-wire fence."

Hammer's face grew black with his inability to sway Dave from such obvious insanity. "You're going to get killed. Only a crazy man would bring in wire to Bear County."

"They've settled the wire-cutters' war down in Texas, Judge. Barbed wire is going to cross-fence all of cattle country before it's all said and done. Someone has to be the first in this county, and I reckon that someone is going to be me."

"You ain't no cattleman!" Hammer shouted. "What's your reason for taking up ranching all of a sudden?"

Dave sighed. "I'm only here to notify you of my residence, Judge. You can mark it in your county records that the Bryant place is back in operation."

The judge appeared on the edge of apoplexy, but he strangled the angry words in his throat and finally lowered his head in defeat. He knew that Dave was going to start a war, but the deed was a legal claim. It was out of his hands.

"All right, Valeron. You win. I'll make a note of your title and also notify the undertaker. There'll be some business headed his way, as sure as you're standing here."

Dave sat the rented horse, memories stirring him as he viewed his old homestead. The ranch house was run down, with the door open and the windows all boarded up. A family of birds was nesting in the overhanging eaves.

The corral was still intact, though two poles were broken and the gate had been torn down. The barn looked usable, with brown straw bales still stacked inside the door.

Dave tied up his horse, walked around the yard, and inspected the house. Using his canteen to prime the pump, he was pleasantly surprised to find that it still worked. He filled the horse trough after getting most of the rusty coloring out of the line. He was about to examine the barn when he heard the approach of a horse. He recognized Big Ed Rutledge at once. The man did not look happy.

"Hot dang, Valeron!" was his less than cordial greeting. "You sure stirred up a hornet's nest, didn't you?"

"What do you mean, Sheriff?" Dave asked, showing a complete innocence.

"You know durned well what I mean! You can't start this place back up!"

"I've got a deed that says it's my spread. I won it fair and square from a young fellow named Bryant. I've already showed the judge my receipt for the back taxes, and the place was never filed on or put up for sale. That makes it my ranch free and clear."

"Bah!" Ed grunted, stretching and arching his back. "Striker will run you out in a week. He ain't going to let his herd die of thirst. It's been a dry fall."

"That's a fact," Dave agreed. "In fact, the drought has burned the grass right out of the fields in a good many places. Except for the natural springs, the water holes are already dry."

"That's just what I'm saying. Striker has no place else to water his stock."

"What about the fall of '76, Ed? Was that a dry year too?"

The sheriff frowned. "What're you getting at?"

"The Bryants were killed that year. Far as I know,

there was never any investigation into their murders.''

"That was twelve years back, Valeron. We didn't
even have a town sheriff then. Someone said it was
a few renegade Sioux Indians. Until now, I always
figured they had taken the boy with them.''

"That's not the way it happened, Ed. Bryant said
it was white men that killed his folks.''

"He should have stuck around and got the U.S.
marshal to do something about it.''

"Considering the way people accepted the death
of his parents, I doubt that he would have lived long
enough to tell anyone much of anything.''

"Well, that there is gone and past. Striker ain't
going to sit back and watch his cattle die of thirst.
No fence is going to ruin a man like him. He's
respected here in Scofield. You won't even have an
ally.''

"I didn't say that I would stop him from watering
his cattle, only that I was going to fence my range.''

Ed's bushy brows knotted in confusion. "So what
does that mean? Talk some sense, Valeron.''

"I'll sell him enough water to take care of his
cattle.''

"Sell water!'' Ed was incredulous. "By glory,
Valeron, I never figured you to be no sidewinding
crook!''

Dave was unmoved by Ed's insult. He knew that
his actions would be unpopular in Scofield. Every-

one would hate him, but he was out to ruin Striker, to strangle him on his own greed, and the shortest route to that end was to take control of the water.

"Striker gained a lot when the Bryants were killed," Dave told Ed. "A more suspicious man than you might have wondered at how quickly he moved in to take over the land and water. He's had it all for free—twelve years of water and land that weren't his. I think it's time he paid a little back for all he's taken."

"I'm a local boy, Valeron, and I don't like outsiders coming in to start a range war. I might decide to look the other way when Striker comes to call on you."

"You do what your conscience tells you to do, Ed. I can handle myself in a fight. You can ask Jake about that."

"A bullet in the back don't allow for any amount of fighting ability. You'd best think hard before you square off against Henry."

"I've already thought it over, Ed. If you try to uphold the law, I'll respect you as a lawman. If you remain neutral, I'll respect you as a man." Dave looked long and hard at Ed. "But if you side against me and the lawful deed I have for this place, I'll forget you even wear a badge."

Ed grunted. "You don't pull punches, I'll give you that."

"I believe in setting down the rules right off. I won't be unreasonable, but I aim to stay."

"You'll end up staying all right—six feet under ground."

Colette heard the rise of angry voices in the kitchen, and she wondered what the men were discussing so hotly so late at night. She had gone to bed an hour earlier, as had Henry and the boys. One of the hands must have brought back news from town that had everyone up and riled.

After slipping on her robe, she tiptoed into the next room, and by standing next to the kitchen door, she could distinguish each man's voice.

Tom was saying, "We can't let him get away with that!"

"He can't do it," Henry replied. "There must be a law that gives us some rights to the water."

"I checked with Judge Hammer," their foreman, Chaps Dawson, said. "He says it's perfectly legal."

"Legal or not, we'll take what we need!" Jake's voice sounded weak as it passed through his swollen lips.

"We're in a fix there, son," Henry said. "If any harm comes to Valeron, Ed will sure enough think we were behind it. Somehow, we have to stay clear of any direct trouble. I don't want to see you behind bars."

"Too bad his water ain't as valuable to Braggs

and his Box Z," Jake muttered. "If we had him behind us, it wouldn't matter what Valeron tried."

"Besides that," Dawson again sounded off, "he has plenty of water and no one would suspect him of any foul play. He doesn't use the grass on the old Bryant spread and he has the stream for watering his cattle. There would be no reason to link him to any accident that happened to Valeron."

"I must remind you men that I'm the Sunday preacher. I can't condone the bodily harm of Valeron. Thou shalt not kill."

"Then you'd best leave the room, Pa." Tom's voice was full of arrogance. "We've got some planning to do."

Henry showed his lack of backbone, and he went out the back door, probably to smoke his pipe. Nowadays he let Jake make the hard decisions and tackle the weighty problems on the place. He had once been a tough, hard man, but Colette had only heard about such things. Ever since she had known him, he was a Bible-thumping sheep, ordered around by his own sons. He let Jake and Tom knock her around, and now, right in his own house, he was letting them plan a killing.

"You got any ideas, Jake?" Tom asked.

"What about Slick Amos?" Dawson said. "He's a lightning-quick gun on Braggs's payroll. How about we get him to take Valeron in a fair fight?"

"That would suit Pa," Tom cried, eager about the idea. "How much would it cost to get him?"

Jake spoke next: "He wouldn't go up against Valeron unless Braggs told him to. He's loyal to the Box Z owner."

"It'd be worth a trip over," Tom said. "Even Pa would go for a fair fight."

Colette silently slipped back into her room. She dared not risk being caught eavesdropping. Once behind the door, she paced the small room like a caged cat. Her stepbrothers were planning Dave Valeron's death. She had to think of some kind of plan to save him.

She wondered what had started everything in motion. There'd been talk about water, but she didn't know what water they referred to. It was something that could harm their ranch but not the Braggs place. The only possible answer was the old, abandoned ranch that lay squarely between the two big spreads.

Colette got into bed, but she wasn't sleepy. She had to think of a way to prevent harm from coming to Dave Valeron. She couldn't sit back and let him be hurt or killed, not after the way he had saved her life and fought for her.

She felt a surge of incredible warmth as she remembered the way that Dave had confronted Jake. He had seemed to take their harsh words and belligerent attitude in stride, until Jake smacked her.

Then he had challenged Jake and soundly thrashed him in a fistfight.

With a firm resolution, Colette decided on a plan of action. She would sneak out and warn Dave of the plot against him. It would be risky, but she had to live with her conscience.

Chapter Five

D ave was up at daybreak, cleaning the house, putting the door back on its hinges, and mending the shutters to close properly. The stove that served for both heating and cooking was salvageable, so he heated coffee and cooked salt pork and beans for his breakfast. He made a mental list of the items he would need to set up house. He was short of about everything imaginable—except for twelve years of dust.

The sound of an approaching horse turned his attention to the yard. He reached for the rifle he had placed next to the door, but recognized Colette Striker and relaxed. A scarf held her hair, and her dress wasn't made for riding. It rode up above her knees, revealing one of several petticoats. He stepped out to meet her, took hold of her horse, and stood ready to help her down.

Colette did not offer to dismount, however. She looked a bit flushed from the ride, and there was concern on her face. Dave figured it meant that trouble was heading his way.

"I guessed that you were up here at the old Bryant shack."

He grinned. "Rundown, maybe, but hardly a shack. It's got three rooms and a workable cookstove. One might consider it a mansion."

"It'll also be your final resting place—mansion *or* shack—if you stay here, Mr. Valeron."

"I'd prefer that you called me Dave."

"I should call you an idiot! Do you realize what you're doing?"

"Yes, ma'am," he drawled. "I know exactly what I am doing, and I didn't come to Scofield to get myself killed."

"Then why are you pitting yourself against the Strikers? You know that they need their water this time of year."

"It isn't their water, Miss Striker," he said with a trace of ire. "The people who owned this ranch were murdered. The Strikers have been using it for free all of these years. It's about time they paid their fair share."

She gave him an imploring look. "But you can't

stand against them all alone. They're planning something terrible.''

''I appreciate that you would risk coming to warn me. I hope you don't get in trouble for it.''

''I'm supposed to be doing the wash. I have to take it down to the edge of the Box Z. No one knows I came to see you.''

''What about your safety? The Butcher tried for you once.''

''I have one of the Mexican riders as my guard. He can be trusted to keep his mouth shut.''

''Again, my thanks for the warning.''

She sat erect in the saddle, defeat visible in her expression. He wished that he dared tell her the whole truth, but it was best to hold back until he had played his hole card.

''Good day, Mr. Valeron,'' she finally said, not accepting his invitation to use his first name. ''I hope you manage to live out the rest of the week.''

He watched her ride away. It would have been nice to invite her in for some lemonade, or to sit in the shade, or possibly to go on an picnic outing. *No room or time for that, not until the debt is paid in full. I sure hope that I'll still be alive for such a time*, he thought.

Axell Braggs had served during the Sioux Indian Wars. He had been a captain at one time, but after being taken captive and tortured for nearly twenty-four hours, he had never been the same. He had resigned his commission shortly after his uncle took ill. The old man died before Axell even got to Scofield to see him. The ranch was now his, and he had slowly regained some of his former self-confidence and strength.

With cool and calculating eyes, he now studied Henry Striker. The man preached the word of God on Sundays, and did whatever he pleased the other days of the week. Axell figured that the odds of Henry's passing through the pearly gates were six-to-one against him.

Personally, Axell had nothing against Henry or his sons. They were careful to return his strays during roundup and never infringed on his property. That might have been more out of fear than friendship, but it didn't really matter. He had the best spread that Montana had to offer, whereas Henry had to scratch and claw to make ends meet each year.

"You have some good hands working for you," Henry was saying like a backyard gossip. "Rat Kingstone, Joe Doley, and Slick Amos. Those are men to ride with, good men in a fight."

"Come to the point, Henry. What do you want from me?"

"Your uncle joined with me in running the Bryant ranch into the ground. Even before they were killed, they were beaten and broke. I'd like to get your help in ridding the land of this new fellow, Valeron.''

''I don't have anything to gain,'' Axell said. ''I use only one canyon on that spread, and that has been to hold a herd overnight during roundup. The land and water have no value to me.''

As Henry ran his fingers through his hair nervously, Axell frowned at the damp circles under his arms. The man was sweating like a shaggy dog in the summer sun. It was unnatural to perspire so readily in fall, when the high temperature was only about seventy degrees. The moisture that wet his shirt was from only one thing—fear.

''But don't you see?'' Henry resumed. ''If we start trouble with Valeron, the law will have to side with him. Like you say, the Box Z has no reason to quarrel with him, so any fighting wouldn't incriminate us.''

''I don't send my men out on killing missions, Striker,'' Axell said curtly. ''If you don't want to face him yourself, hire a killer.''

''I can't do that. I have to stand in front of the people on Sunday mornings. I have to be able to look them in the eye.''

''What am I supposed to do about your personal problem, Henry? I'm a businessman, a respected man in the community. I have nothing to gain from making war on Valeron.''

Henry was determined to win the man over.

"Maybe we could strike a deal of some kind. What do you want, Braggs? What price would it take to have you handle the whole thing and me not know about it at all?"

"You sound like a desperate man."

"I stand to lose my entire herd if I don't have access to that water. There must be something of value that I have, something that would encourage you to help me out."

Axell rubbed a scar on his chin. "You do have something, but I don't know how you would feel about giving it to me."

"Anything, Axell."

"I'll take Colette, the young lady on your ranch."

Henry looked at him in amazement. "You want my stepdaughter as your wife?"

"Well, I certainly don't need another house-keeper. What do you say to that?"

Henry thought as fast as his mind would function. He had the power to say whom Colette was going to marry. Why not promise her to Axell? He was the most wealthy and powerful man in a hundred miles. There was no reason not to give her hand to him, and it would cement a lasting union between the two ranches. In the end, Jake and Tom could inherit all of Bear County.

"Consider it done, Axell. You rid the land of Dave Valeron, and I'll announce the engagement of

Colette to you at a Sunday meeting. We can set the wedding date after that.''

The two men shook hands to seal the bargain. As Henry left the ranch, Axell watched him ride away and felt a growing excitement. His heart began to hammer in his chest. He envisioned Colette in white, standing at his side, being addressed as Mrs. Braggs. It was enough to stir long-forgotten feelings.

Dave was mending the corral, his rifle close at hand, when he saw three riders coming up the trail toward the main house. About to reach for the weapon, he recognized the floppy-tailed coonskin cap of Pecos Thorn. The two men with him would be Short Loop Moleen and Concho Mestas, two knowledgeable cattlemen who knew also how to handle a gun in a fight.

Doubt shadowed Dave's mind as he saw the three of them coming his way. He was in this game for revenge, but the others were in it for profit. He had to make certain this panned out for them, even if he didn't make a dime himself.

Pecos was well along in years, waiting for age to put an end to his travel and hardworking days. He wanted to set down roots and toy at odd jobs during his twilight years. Dave knew that the man had no stomach for this fight, but he was a loyal friend and more of a father to him than his natural one had ever

been. He would be at Dave's side, whether invited
or not.

The three men stopped at the corral and Concho
dropped to the ground. His ready smile greeted
Dave, and he said, "I'll help you with that there
gate, so we can put up the horses. We'll be needing
a place to hold the cattle too."

"There's a box canyon that borders the Box Z
range. We can run them in there and throw up a
barricade across the mouth to hold them. It ought to
feed a hundred head for a few days. Only thing,
we'll have to let them water daily."

"Is the water near the mouth of the canyon?"

"Right close."

Pecos dismounted slowly, stiff from the long
hours in the saddle. He arched his back, both hands
on his hips.

"Durned if it ain't a long haul up here, Davy.
Hope I don't have to pull many guard shifts. I'm
getting along in years, you know."

Concho laughed. "He's so old that he gets winded
just wrestling with temptation."

"Yeah," Short Loop jumped in. "When he asks
a gal for a dance, he hopes she says no!"

"Couple of young wiseacres we brung with us,
Davy. Was a time that I'd have taken the both of
them on together, with one hand tied behind my
back."

Concho laughed. "Now he couldn't take the two

of us if we had both of our hands tied behind *our* backs!''

Dave smiled at the joshing. The three men were good to have around. They worked well as a team and always had something going to laugh about. He would need that, a kinship or bond between them.

''You speak to Judge Hammer yet?'' Pecos had turned serious.

''He ranted and yelled for five minutes, but everything is legal. This place is ours. I've already had a visit from Big Ed Rutledge, the sheriff of Scofield. He warned me, Judge Hammer warned me, and Colette Striker warned me.''

Pecos took notice of the last name. ''What'd you say—Colette Striker? Who is she?''

''Henry took a second wife a few years back. Colette is his stepdaughter. She's a beauty, Pecos. After meeting her, I almost forgot why I wanted to come back here . . . until I met up with Jake, that is.''

Pecos grinned. ''Don't see no black eye or lumps. Did you mix it up yet?''

Dave looked down and raised his hands. He rubbed the palm of his left hand over his right knuckles. ''We crossed tracks and I ran over him.''

''You got something to beat on this gate with?''

Concho interrupted the conversation. "The old hinge is about bent in two."

"We need to get some supplies from town. We're short of about everything."

Concho held up his hand. "Don't you worry none, boss. Me and Short Loop will run in and buy everything we need. We ought to get a look at the town before everyone in it starts to hate us."

Concho grinned as he spoke, but Dave knew he was correct. The dark-haired, bronze-skinned Concho, and the taciturn, seldom-smiling Short Loop would be targets of ridicule as soon as word spread about his taking over the Bryant place.

"How long till the cattle arrive?" Dave asked.

"Maybe three days," Pecos answered. "It ain't long enough to get all the work done."

"We'll have time to organize a little. No one knows about the cattle yet."

Pecos sighed. He was weary but ready to get started. "It's your game, son. You set down the rules and that's the way we'll play."

"Can't argue with that kind of cooperation." Dave dug into his pocket and pulled out some money. "Here you go, Concho. You and Short Loop get on into town. Pick up a week's supply of grub, some extra blankets, tools, and the like. Remember that it gets colder here than in Wyoming."

"What about you and Pecos? What are you two going to do?"

"We'll pay a neighborly visit to the nearby ranches. No need having any confusion over what we intend to do."

Concho touched the butts of the two matched .45s on his hips. "Maybe you ought to send Pecos with Short Loop. If trouble starts, you might need some help."

The old man glared at Concho. "I've forgotten more about the art of gunplay or fighting than you'll ever live long enough to learn."

Pecos's flare-up put a grin on the young man's face. "Yeah, that's the trouble, Pecos. You've *forgotten* most of it!"

Pecos muttered and growled to himself while Concho mounted his horse. Even as Concho and Short Loop rode off, he continued to complain.

"Someday, Davy, someday I'm going to have to trim that boy's mustache. He's more conceited than a lone rooster in a chicken coop full of hens."

"Reminds you of yourself at about the same age, huh?"

Pecos's gruff exterior changed at once. He smiled. "Durned if it don't, Davy. Durned if it don't."

"Shadow was killed out from under me." Dave clenched a hand. "You probably noticed that the horse in the corral is an old nag."

Pecos squinted at the animal. "I was about to

ask what happened to Shadow. That was a fine steed.''

"There's a maniac running loose in the valley. He has murdered three young women in the past few months."

Pecos's eyes grew wide. "What kind of crazed lunatic would do something like that?"

"I can't imagine what goes on in the sick brain of such a ruthless butcher."

"And you say this varmint killed your horse?"

Dave told him about the attack and the subsequent fight with Jake Striker.

"Real gratitude," Pecos said. "I always knew them Strikers were a bunch of mangy coyotes. I remember the way Henry used to run the entire valley. Even Roger Braggs avoided him, and he owned a spread that was twice the size of Striker's."

"Roger died some time back. His nephew, Axell, is running the Box Z."

"What do you know about him?"

"Not much. He was in the war against the Sioux and took over the ranch after his uncle died. I don't know what to expect from him."

"I expect our trouble will be with Henry Striker. He was always the bull of the woods here in Bear County."

"His son Jake seems to be the new boss of the family. Jake was more in control than Henry—it was his mouth that did the talking."

Pecos frowned. "That's sure odd. Henry was an iron fist when you and I left the valley. Wonder what happened to him?"

"Doesn't really matter to me," Dave said firmly. "I came to run the entire family into the ground, and that includes all three men."

"What about this here gal Colette?"

Dave couldn't answer that. "We'll see about her when the time comes."

Chapter Six

Colette sucked in her breath. Surprised, she looked squarely into Chaps Dawson's thin face. His narrow features were those of a ferret, and his beady black eyes flashed in the light. He stepped past Colette and rubbed his hand along the shoulder of her horse.

"Been doing some hard riding this morning, Miss Striker. Where've you been?"

"I don't have time to chew the fat, Dawson," she replied haughtily, trying to bluff her way past him. "I've got baking to do."

But the hired hand grabbed hold of her wrist and jerked her along after him, pulling her toward the house.

"Maybe we ought to let Henry know what you

been up to. He worries about you, what with that killer running loose.''

Colette's heart began to pound. She swallowed the fear that rose in her throat and tried to remain calm. Unable to fight against Dawson's superior strength, she went along with him.

Jake was the one to greet them. Still furious from his beating, he was looking for a way to strike back at someone. He had a wicked sneer on his swollen lips.

''Where you been, Sparrow? You been flying around the countryside again?''

Henry must have heard him, for he appeared at the doorway of the house. His horse was tied at the hitch post, sweat-stained from a hard morning's ride. Suspicion was strong in his expression.

''Let's hear it, gal!'' he demanded. ''You didn't take any laundry with you, so you darn certain didn't do no washing.''

Colette was trapped by her own eagerness to warn Dave Valeron. She realized that she should have done some washing to cover her trip. Instead of denying her actual purpose, she took a deep breath and faced her stepfather.

''You know where I went, Mr. Striker. I rode over to warn Mr. Valeron that his life was in danger.''

Jake took hold of his belt and began to unbuckle it. ''That's it, Sparrow! I'm going to whale the daylights out of you. Tom! Come out here and tie Colette to the gate. It's time we taught her a lesson.''

Tom joined them on the porch, but Henry held up his hand to stop his two sons. He put on his judgmental face, the one he used on Sunday to commence calling everyone sinners. He took a step forward and glared at Colette.

"Why would you sell us out? Why would you sell out your own family?"

"I didn't sell anyone out, Mr. Striker. I repaid Mr. Valeron for saving my life. You and the boys treated him like a criminal after he risked his very life to save me from the Butcher. I felt that I owed him a debt. I rode over to the old Bryant place and told him that his life was in danger."

"What about us?" he asked. "How can we survive if he takes our water? Don't you care about anyone else?"

Colette took a deep breath and said boldly, "You preach brotherly love on Sunday, Mr. Striker. Then you let Jake attack a man who saved me from certain death. I felt it my duty to return payment of some kind to Mr. Valeron. We are even now, for I warned him that his life was in danger."

"Enough of this chatter," Jake jeered. "Take hold of her, Tom."

Then Henry did something that Colette had never seen him do before. He planted himself bodily between her and the boys. His hands rested on his hips, blocking the way.

"There'll be no punishment this time, Jake. Colette was possessed to do her Christian duty, and I suppose we did owe Valeron a debt for saving her life. We can now consider that debt paid in full."

"She sneaked off to another man, Pa!" Jake was livid. "You can't turn the other cheek this time. She went against her own family!"

But Henry would not move. "I've said there will be no punishment this time. I don't put my foot down often, but this time I have no choice. Let me handle it, Jake. I have our best interests in mind."

Jake swore under his breath and hobbled back into the house. Tom had a puzzled look on his face, but he also left the porch. After Chaps returned to work, only Henry and Colette remained.

She was amazed that her stepfather had taken up against Jake. It was the first time in her memory that he had ever done that. When he looked at her, she saw a much older man. His hair was graying, and there were deep circles under his eyes and thick lines at the corners of his mouth. He was drained of strength, exhausted from the confrontation.

"I'm very glad that you understand my feelings, Mr. Striker."

He did not respond to her statement, and said instead, "You are of marrying age, and I've been looking for a proper suitor." He let the words sink in. "If not for your mother changing your name to Striker, I should have wanted you to marry Tom or Jake."

Colette gave a silent prayer of thanks to her mother for that, but showed only an impassive, patient look to Henry. A foreboding grew like a shadow, covering her with an instant darkness. She was fearful of her stepfather's next words.

"A father is responsible for picking a good provider for his daughter, a man who'll have a lot to offer. I've chosen the best man in the valley for you, Colette. It was not an easy task to arrange, but you're to marry Axell Braggs."

Colette was too stunned to speak. She had seen Axell only from a distance at Sunday meetings. To her recollection, she had never spoken a word to him.

"But. . . ."

Henry again held up his hand for silence. "I have made the decision, Colette. We'll announce your engagement one of these Sundays, and the two of you will have a chance to get acquainted. There'll be no discussion or argument."

He left her standing there, bewildered, her mind scrambled, her body feeling somehow tormented physically. *I'm to marry Axell Braggs! I don't even know him! I know nothing about him.* She crossed her arms and hugged herself timorously, like a frightened child. Her fate was much more frightening than the beating Jake had proposed.

Dave and Pecos might have saved their efforts. Each place was the same. He was regarded as an interloper, a greedy troublemaker. Henry had few close friends, but he preached on Sunday and read from the Good Book. There was no warmth or greeting for the men who had come to Scofield to deprive him of water and land.

Axell was not at his house, so their trip was wasted on that ride. When they entered the yard at the Striker spread, only Mrs. Striker was there, and she was not eager to speak or show any hospitality towards them.

"I thank you for saving my daughter's life," she said as they were about to leave. "I hoped you would take her warning and leave the valley. She risked a great deal by riding over to see you."

Dave's interest sharpened. "Henry knows about it?"

"One of the hired men caught her returning with a lathered horse and no laundry. It didn't take a lot of pondering to determine where she'd gone. Jake wanted to use a belt on her, and it's a wonder Henry prevented him from beating her to within an inch of her life."

A raw hatred filled Dave to his very soul. "If one of those men raises a hand to her ever again, I'll kill him, Mrs. Striker.'' His words were so forceful that the woman's eyes widened.

''A man has the right to discipline his own daughter—be it a stepchild or not.''

''Discipline is not beating them with a strap—not at Colette's age. She's a young woman, not some naughty brat who needs a spanking. You're her mother. Don't you have any compassion for your own daughter?''

''You're the cause of the trouble, Mr. Valeron. You've brought nothing but grief to the valley. You probably don't know it yet, but your actions have determined my daughter's fate. You're responsible for everything that will happen from this time forward. I hope you can live with that.'' She gnashed her teeth. ''I hope my Colette can live with that!''

He had no idea what she meant, but before he could question her, she rushed into the house and slammed the door.

''Nothing like palavering with the neighbors,'' Pecos said with a grin. ''Makes your heart glad when you see all this here brotherly love at work.''

''I figured Colette's mother would be an ally, but she seems to hate me with the same passion as the rest of the Strikers.''

''Maybe she ain't partial to bloodsuckers, son.''

''I suppose that's exactly how we look, Pecos. I didn't expect anyone to be overjoyed about my return.''

"Well, I think I can safely say that you're right about that. If you were the Black Death on horseback, you'd have gotten the same warm reception."

"Let's head on back to the ranch. We've got work to do."

Pecos chuckled. "Yeah, no need making any more friends today. We'll be getting all swell-headed by so many people making a fuss over us."

Chapter Seven

Dave mopped his brow and looked down the row of fence posts. The three of them were making good progress. Concho was good with a shovel, and Short Loop was a magician with an ax, cutting poles for posts as fast as Dave and Concho could ready a hole. Pecos had a load of wire down at the house, and he brought out lunch and prepared the evening meal.

"Been at it three days," Concho remarked as they stopped to take a breather. "We'll have the fence put up to shut out Striker's cattle by late tomorrow. Kind of worries me that there's been no sign of him."

"I know what you mean," Dave told him. "I

71

expected a fire, an attack by some of his men, something. I can't see him taking this without a fight.''

"Think he knows about the cattle coming in?''

"I doubt it.''

"They ought to arrive sometime tomorrow.''

"With this much fence put up, we shouldn't have to hold them in the canyon for more than a few days. We can save some of that feed for wintering.''

"Might need it too. The drought has charred a lot of natural grass. I don't recall ever seeing Montana look so dry.''

"It's spooky all right.''

"What about your budding romance?'' Concho asked with a laugh. "You haven't been sneaking out at nights to some rendezvous. What happened to the fire between you and that Striker girl?''

"I can't put her in danger. If she was caught seeing me, her family would whip her, and then I'd ride in and kill the lot of them. That would likely get a rope around my neck.''

"I suppose some men think that the belt is the only way to teach a kid to walk the straight and narrow.''

Dave grinned. "Didn't work with you, did it?''

Concho laughed, but there was no humor in his expression. "My pa was from that school of thought, Dave. He swung a leather belt and used it frequently. When I was sixteen, I took the belt away from him.'' He shrugged. "Discipline is needed for all kids, but it has to be mixed equally with love. I don't recall my pa ever saying one kind word to me."

Dave shook his head. "My own father was gruff and as hard as a railroad spike, but I can't recall any beatings."

"There's a surefire way to see that your gal don't get a belt used on her, Dave. Just say the word, and we'll settle this whole affair up front. A fair fight would satisfy that judge in town."

Dave considered his suggestion. "I've given it some thought, Concho. Do you think I was wrong to take the long way around in getting even with the Strikers?"

"Could be. You want to mix revenge in with justice. Me and Short Loop understand your reasons. If this pans out, Striker will bend and crack before he falls to his knees. He made you suffer ten years and you want to repay him for them."

"Pecos thinks I'll end up bitter and empty once I've crushed them into the dirt."

Concho grinned once more. "Shucks, you'll probably get killed long before that time comes."

"Might get everyone around me killed as well, Concho. You ever think about that?"

"The surveyor must've thought along those lines, because he staked this range quicker than I ever seen one of those fellows work before. He was here and gone before anyone got to know his name."

Dave smiled, but then tipped his head toward a

number of cattle. They were moving between the posts, wading the mud to reach the water in some nearby beaver ponds. He told Concho, "When we string wire, we'll have cattle milling up against the fence twenty-four hours a day. I don't like watching them suffer. They didn't ask to belong to a worthless tyrant like Striker."

"The watering holes I've seen on his place are either dust or too alkaline to drink. Usually, there's a little rain by this time of the year, but I ain't seen a cloud in weeks."

"There's other sign too," Dave agreed. "Wild geese, ducks, and songbirds have already cleared out of the high country. And the beaver ponds have more willow saplings piled in for the winter than I've ever seen before."

"If you can believe Pecos, the muskrat lodges were twice their usual size too. He told me that he spotted one of those arctic owls up in the hills yesterday. I don't recall ever seeing one in Montana before."

"It's practically November and no rain. Could mean one tough winter ahead when it finally arrives."

Concho looked up at the cloudless sky. "Might be a real hard year, Dave. Nature might want to bury us under six feet of snow and the Strikers will want to bury us under six feet of earth."

"Still time to pack your gear and ride. This isn't your fight."

Concho laughed at the suggestion. "Shucks, Dave, I don't have anything else to do. Might as well stick here and share the fun."

Henry was exasperated, angry, and confused all at once, because Axell had not fulfilled their bargain.

"We shook hands on it! We had a deal!" Henry yelled at the other rancher.

Axell was impassive, unwilling to bend or to relent. He puffed on a strong-smelling cigar, then purposely blew the smoke in Henry's direction. The smoke worsened the already unsatisfactory situation.

"One man was the deal, Henry. You said we only had to deal with Valeron. You claimed he was fencing you off from your rightful watering holes. Now I discover that he owns that property legally and is bringing in his own herd of cattle."

Henry was shocked at the latter bit of news. He hadn't heard of any cattle. Still, he remained steadfast and to the point.

"What difference does that make? Our deal hasn't changed basically."

"I have word that his men look capable. I admit that Colette is a worthwhile prize, but I don't want a full-scale war on my hands. How much money is behind Valeron? How many more men are coming with the herd to join him? Are they willing to fight?

Those are important considerations in a campaign such as this.''

Henry rubbed his hands together, and then his brow furrowed. ''What would it take to get you into this battle?''

Axell ran a finger along the scar on his chin thoughtfully. He took another long puff on the cigar and then stared at the burning end.

''Colette is fine as a part of our deal. However, if I'm to enter into a range war, I'll need other compensation.'' He looked at Henry as if measuring how much he could ask. ''Half of your cattle, Henry,'' he said at last. ''That's my price—Colette and half of your herd.''

''What?'' Henry cried. ''Great sunrise in the morning, Axell! Are you crazy?''

Axell smiled at his cigar. ''You're the one who wants help. I have nothing to gain in starting a range war. It's the lives of my men and cattle that are expected to be on the line, not yours. If I take the risk, I expect suitable payment.''

Henry was up and pacing, hands locked at his back. The demand was totally unreasonable, but what other choices did he have? Big Ed might side with Valeron if he took action himself. After all, Valeron did have a legal claim. He might oppose Striker, but he wouldn't dare stand against Axell too. To fight alone might be to lose everything.

''I'll give you five hundred head of cattle,'' he

countered the offer. ''Along with that, you have my permission to marry Colette straightaway.''

Axell considered the offer for what seemed an eternity to Henry. Then he blew another puff of smoke, nodded, and said, ''Plus, I take the cattle that Valeron is bringing in. I'm informed that they're Herefords.''

''Cows are cows,'' Henry said, the bitter taste of the ruthless bargaining still in his mouth. ''You get his herd too. Is it a deal?''

''We have reached agreement, Henry. Today is October the twenty-second. I'll expect our wedding for the first week of November.''

''All right, if that's the way you want it.''

Axell showed a smug, twisted grin. ''That's the way I want it.''

Henry left the room in an angry mood. He hated to part with five hundred head of cattle and then let Axell also take Valeron's herd. The man was a crook and had taken advantage of the situation. One day he might let Jake even the score that was mounting between them. Jake was strong and sure. Once he healed up from his beating, he would again make the decisions. That was something Henry wanted no more of, the deciding who lived and who died.

Dave remained back in the trees, watching until Striker and his sons rode out of the yard. The crew had left shortly after sunup, so the place was almost deserted. He would have to watch out only for Colette's mother and possibly a hired man.

He rode his mount through the brush and trees, weaving a path to the rear of the house. He approached to within fifty yards and tied off his horse in a hollow. Then he crossed the distance to the house, swiftly and unseen.

At the side of the house he listened at a window for sounds of people stirring. At the kitchen door, he saw Colette's mother exit the front door of the house. From his position, he had not been able to see that there was a horse and buggy ready and waiting on the far side of the yard.

"I'll be back in a couple of hours," he heard the woman say. "Anything else that you can think of?"

"No, Mother. I'll start the laundry as soon as I get this dress sewn up."

"Watch for any strangers and keep the shotgun handy. No telling where the Butcher is at."

"I'll be careful."

Dave watched the woman get into the buggy. Once she was out of the yard, he slipped inside the house.

Colette was sitting with her back toward the door of her room. Dave leaned against the frame, watching her nimble fingers run a needle through some white material. She was dressed in the tattered cotton dress she had been wearing during her visit to his ranch. Her hair was combed loosely down to her shoulders, and she had one leg crossed over the other as she worked. He hated to frighten her, but it was not proper to spy on her, either.

"If I was the Butcher, you'd be at my mercy, Miss Striker."

Though he spoke the words softly, she gasped in alarm and dropped her sewing at her feet. Her recognition of him calmed her at once, but there could be no doubt that anything sudden or unexpected would panic her.

"What are you doing here?" she asked, nervously looking out the window of the room. "If Henry or. . . ."

"I was careful," he replied, trying to put her fears to rest. "I've been watching the place for some time."

She regarded him with those gray-blue eyes, openly curious and magnetically inviting. He held himself in check, fighting down the temptation to move closer.

"Then you know that I'm alone in the house. Why did you come?"

He felt a loss of confidence and words. "I . . . I wanted to see you," he managed weakly. "I thought you might have gotten into trouble for warning me the other day."

She did not meet his scrutiny, and put her attention on her sewing once more. "Mr. Striker agreed that the act made us even. You saved my life and I warned you.''

''Real Christian of him,'' he said sarcastically. ''Maybe I ought to come to church next Sunday and listen to one of his sermons.''

She stopped any pretense of sewing. ''Then you would be present to hear the announcement of my forthcoming marriage to Axell Braggs.''

Dave's heart sank inside his chest, settling there like a bullet in still water. He worked hard to get his brain to function.

''I rode up to see him the other day, but he wasn't at the ranch.'' Dave struggled to conceal his agony at the news. ''Is he a good man?''

''I've never spoken to him,'' she replied. ''I've seen him at church and once or twice in town. I believe he's about fifteen years older than I am, but he'd be a good provider for our children.''

That twisted like a knife in Dave's gut. He discovered that his hands were tightly knotted into fists, and he struggled to keep the fury and anguish out of his voice. ''You can't possibly have any real feelings for the man,'' he murmured. ''Do you think you'll learn to love him?''

She didn't look up at him. ''It makes no difference. The date has been set for the wedding. I'll be his wife by the end of the first week of November.''

Dave crossed the remaining distance between them. He took hold of her arms, forcing her to drop her sewing once more. She looked up at him. Her eyes misted with tears. Regret was plain on her face.

"You don't want to marry him, do you?"

"I have no choice. I'm a Striker and Henry owns my life. Only he has the say as to who I marry."

He lifted her up out of the chair and, without thinking, he drew her into his arms. He kissed her hard, giving vent to his anger and boiling turmoil. When her lips responded, he quickly relented. There was a desperation in her reaction. He could feel her fear and apprehension, her uncertainty and dread.

He summoned the strength to push her away. She began sobbing into her hands. He had no idea if it was from shame or hopeless frustration.

"I'll not stand by and see you forced into a life of bondage, Colette. If there's any way to prevent your marrying Axell Braggs, I'll find it. I promise you, I'll find a way."

She came into his arms and buried her face against his chest. He had made a big promise, a string of words that might be impossible to back up with actions. A father had the say in whom his daughter married. It had been that way forever. The law was on Striker's side. But he vowed:

Somehow, some way, I've got to stop the wedding. I want Colette for my own!

Chapter Eight

Judge Hammer peered at Dave as if he were a crazy man. "You want to do what?" he muttered.

"I want to prevent Colette Striker from being forced to marry Axell Braggs."

"What business is it of yours?"

"The girl doesn't even know the man, Judge. Besides, he's nearly twice her age."

Hammer drew his bushy brows together. "Why should that matter to you? Do you have designs of your own on the young lady?"

Dave hated the knowing look that came into the man's eyes. "Just tell me about the law, Judge. Is there some legal way to stop such a union?" he asked.

''The lawful guardian of a child has the right of consent for that child. A girl is bound by such word until she reaches the age of twenty-one. Unless she has the courage to refuse Axell right at the ceremony, I don't think that. . . .''

The judge stopped suddenly, as if struck by some vague thought.

''What is it?'' Dave asked.

Hammer frowned in deep concentration. ''Let's pull up the team and let the animals blow for a spell, Valeron.'' He regarded Dave with a piercing gaze. ''There might be another angle here, but first I've got to know a few things.''

''Such as?''

''Word has it that you're bringing in a herd of cattle to the Bryant place. Also, I saw a familiar face in town yesterday, the face of Pecos Thorn.'' He looked Dave up one way and back again. ''I was good friends with Sam Bryant before he was killed. You have a strong resemblance to the Bryant boy who disappeared the night Sam died. Am I getting warm?''

Dave let out a sigh. ''You're on fire, Judge. I'm Dave Bryant.''

''Took me a little time to think this out, but I got to wondering about the deed and the taxes always being paid by a third party. It has taken me a few days to figure the angles. I thought you had come back for revenge, but now you've got a herd of cattle. Maybe you'd care to shed some light on your plans.''

"I came back for revenge plain and simple. But once I arrived, I decided to settle for justice. Meeting up with Colette was something I hadn't counted on.''

"I know the facts surrounding your parents' deaths, son. In fact, I know more about that incident than even you do.''

Dave wondered what the judge meant by that. He had found his mother dead and had watched from the window as Henry Striker shot and killed his father. What more did he need to know?

"The same thing is true of Colette and her mother,'' Hammer was saying. "I could use that information to give her a choice about marrying Axell Braggs.''

"What about my parents' deaths?''

The judge's lips pressed into a thin line. "Some skeletons are better left buried, Dave. Suffice to say, I'm on your side when it comes to your holding the land your folks owned. Don't ask more of me than that. I never liked Henry Striker, but I have a degree of respect for him.''

There was no point in pestering Hammer, for he was as tough as his name. If he said that that was all he would tell Dave, then that was all he would tell him.

"What about Colette Striker? What do I have to do?''

The judge grinned. "I'll explain it to you, son. See what you think."

Dave left the judge's office, which was the front room of his house, about fifteen minutes later. He now had to pick up some fasteners and nails for the fence wire that was being strung. He crossed the street, for the general store was directly opposite the judge's place. As he entered the store, he caught sight of two Box Z horses tied to a nearby hitching post.

Dave continued into the store, but he turned at the window and surveyed the street. As he had feared, the two Box Z men were watching the store intently. He didn't know either of them, but he recognized them as trouble.

Makes sense, he told himself. *Braggs and Striker have joined forces to keep me out. The wedding to Colette is likely the sealing of some kind of deal between them. Question is, how far are they willing to go to stop me?*

He ordered the nails and fasteners and then took them out to his horse and strapped them on behind the saddle. He didn't have time to mount, for one of the two Box Z men soon approached him.

Dave took note of the man, of the way his hand was close to his gun. He wore the holster tied low on his hip for a quick draw. Dave used to practice getting his own gun out, for endless hours, under the watchful eye of Pecos Thorn. As much time as he had spent boxing, he had even more hours working with a gun.

"Valeron?" the man asked, eyeing him cautiously.

"That's me," Dave replied. "Something I can do for you, friend?"

As he spoke the words, Dave moved a step away from his horse, his own hand near his gun. Thinking ahead, he had already removed the thong from the hammer of his Colt Peacemaker. Pecos had warned him that a man's muscles would tense an instant before he drew his gun. To survive a gunfight, a man had to be ready to shoot to kill, to react at once. His senses were at a peak, every nerve on edge.

"I've got a proposition for you, Valeron."

"That so?"

The man nodded, his cold yellow-brown eyes steady. As poised as a snake, he was in a fighting stance though not yet in a crouch.

"You can take your men and cattle from the valley. Ride far and long, and don't stop until you're a hundred miles from here. No reason for anyone to get hurt over a tiny parcel of land."

"What does my land have to do with the Box Z? We only border your holdings. We have no quarrel with you."

The man ignored the question. "Them are the only terms you're going to get. Take them and live"—

his face muscles tightened, his voice turned to frost—"or refuse them and die."

Dave did not budge, and flicked a glance over at the second man. His arms were crossed. He was there only to watch.

"That's a tough choice," Dave said, "but I think I'll refuse the offer. I'm here to stay."

A sneer curled the man's lips. "You called the shot, Valeron. Where would you like it—between your eyes?"

Dave tensed. Butterflies the size of bats fluttered inside his gut, and his heart pounded uncontrollably. He was acutely alert, with his nerves coiled like a tightly wound watch spring. "Whatever you're being paid, it isn't enough, fella. I'm no green amateur with a gun."

The man took two deliberate steps back, as if wanting a certain distance to be comfortable. His confidence showed in his eyes as he sneered at Dave with open contempt.

"Makes it all the more fun, Valeron. I hate to shoot a man while his gun is still in its holster."

Dave did not reply to that, waiting, watching, ready to draw. . . .

It was a blur, the darting of hands toward guns, the smooth, practiced action making the guns materialize in both Dave's hand and that of the other man at the same instant.

The gun recoiled in Dave's hand, the blast going

off a microsecond before that of the other man. The bullet struck his opponent in the left side of his chest, knocking his aim enough so that his own bullet whistled past Dave's right ear and smashed into the wall of the hardware store.

Dave held his gun cocked and ready to fire a second time. But the man was stunned and lowering his weapon. His eyes were open wide in shock and surprise, and so was his mouth. He was incredulous that Dave had beaten him to the draw.

"D-dang, Valeron . . ." he grunted as his gun slipped from numb fingers. "Y-you are . . . are . . . fast!" He sagged to his knees, one hand over the crimson blotch on his shirt. Disbelief and horror were on his face. Then his features went slack and he fell forward, dead in the street.

Dave retained sense enough to aim his gun at the second Box Z man. No hostility showed as the fellow came up to examine the body of the other one. He had been only a spectator.

"Slick Amos was supposed to be the best man around with a gun," he said after checking the downed man for a pulse. "Guess he wasn't so all-fired quick as he claimed."

"I don't want any trouble with the Box Z," Dave told him. "You tell that to your boss."

There was a new light of respect in the man's eyes. "I'll pass that along, Valeron."

Several other people approached the scene of the

fight, with Judge Hammer leading the way. He looked upset by the episode, but his voice was cool and professional when he spoke:

"I witnessed the fight, Valeron. It won't take a court of law to declare this self-defense, but what caused it? Why should the Box Z send their champion gunman against you?"

Dave tipped his head toward the man kneeling at Amos's side. "Ask the other fellow here."

But the judge didn't speak, because Big Ed was hurrying up the street. Ed looked from the dead man to Dave.

"I knew it! I knew you'd be nothing but trouble!"

The judge took Ed aside to explain what had happened, and Dave didn't wait around. He mounted his horse and rode out of town. It was going to take some time to calm his shattered nerves. He had never killed a man before. There was no glory, no satisfaction at winning a fight, only relief at surviving. He felt sick inside, and knew that Slick Amos would haunt his dreams for the rest of his life.

The lights of the house had been off for two hours. The Butcher sat in the darkness and thought of his foolhardiness in coming to the Striker ranch. He could not very well slip in and abduct the girl from her room. That would be nearly impossible.

He wondered about seeing the judge there earlier.

Was he warning them to be wary? Did he have some information about the killings?

Those were the scattered fears of a man who knew that his luck would one day run out. The judge knew nothing about him. It was possible that he had come out to see Henry, to warn him off, to try to prevent more trouble between Valeron and the other two ranches. Still, the judge had spoken directly to Mrs. Striker, not Henry. That was a puzzle.

He shook the unimportant thoughts from his head. With the cunning that only a madman could know, and the stealth of a wolf seeking helpless prey, he threaded his path down through the trees.

He paused near the tack shed and watched and listened. He was not the kind of man to attack in a panic, caught up in some sort of frenzy. He was deliberate, careful, and, most of all, patient.

Standing in the shadows, the Butcher used his keen senses to test the sounds and sights of the night. He padded softly over to the side of the house. His movements were so quiet and smooth that even the nearby dogs were unaware of his presence.

He slipped over to the window. It was open a crack, but the room was totally dark. He sniffed the air like the part-animal that drove him, and he detected the scent of a woman's shampoo. The sweet fragrance was strong, and he willed his eyes to penetrate the blackness enough to see the dim outline of a white robe next to the bed.

Ever so silently, like a snake slithering through high, wet grass, he opened the window and eased into the room.

His hand produced his long skinning knife while he searched the bed with eyes that steadily grew more accustomed to the dark. He could see the bundles beneath the covers, as if the girl were having a restless night. He perceived the hair against the pillow, the black, silken hair. Carefully, he poised over the form, his knife raised to strike. He would not make her suffer, would not allow her a single sound. It had to be a quick and deadly thrust.

As the knife plunged downward, he was stupefied to see a second person in the bed.

"Wha . . . ?" the groggy man grunted.

The Butcher jerked the knife from the woman's body, and then he slashed at the sleepy-eyed man. But the man was quick to react. He threw himself off the bed and out of reach.

"Help!" he cried. "Boys!"

The Butcher realized his error at once. He had gotten into the old man's room. He had just killed Sela Striker!

Voices were raised in excitement throughout the house, but the Butcher dived out the window. The dogs barked excitedly as he raced for the trees. Gunfire cracked through the night. The bullets were shot in haste, and the elusive target was fleet and agile, and he was into the trees before any of the shots could find their mark. He cursed his stupidity as he ran, for he had missed Colette a second time.

Chapter Nine

Dave stood to the back of the small crowd of people, remaining inconspicuous. He was able to see the proceedings, but it was Colette he mainly kept his eye on. She was pale from the strain, grief-stricken by the horrible murder of her mother.

Dave had only managed to learn a few of the details, but he did know that the woman was killed in her bed while asleep. She had not suffered, for she had never known of the attack. It was small consolation.

Tom Striker worked his way through the crowd and stopped in front of Dave. He put his hands on his hips and thrust his jaw forward in hate.

"What're you doing here, Valeron? No one asked you to come!"

"I'm paying my respects, that's all."

"We don't want your respects," Tom sneered. "Why don't you go play with your stinking cattle!"

"The cattle are penned, all fenced nice and secure."

"Don't you bet on how long they stay that way."

"You're free to drive your cattle down to water. One cent a head each day they water. I told your pa my terms."

"We ain't paying nothing for your water."

Dave looked up at the clear sky. "You might be saved by a winter storm, but I don't think you should count on it. Those cattle haven't had decent water in a week. It'll be better to pay the price than lose the entire herd."

"Jake will tend to you, Valeron. You were lucky against him last time, but it won't happen again. Soon as he's ready, we'll take care of you and your cattle."

Dave didn't respond because he wanted to avoid an argument at a funeral. He took the threat in stride, then found a sturdy-looking, flinty-eyed man standing in front of him. The man had a cigar clenched between his teeth, but it wasn't lit. He appraised Dave with a short, all-inclusive glance.

"You're Dave Valeron?"

"That's right."

"I'm Axell Braggs, owner of the Box Z."

"Should I be impressed or intimidated?"

Braggs's eyes were chips of ice. "You killed a good man the other day. Slick Amos was one of my top hands."

"You took the chance when you sent him to challenge me to a fight. I rode out to your ranch to tell you that I wanted no trouble, but you weren't at home. I'll tell you now to your face, I want no fight with the Box Z."

"You've antagonized everyone in the valley, Valeron. Slick was trying to do a community service."

"I'm only asking for what's rightly mine. I own the Bryant spread, and I intend to use the land and water as I see fit.

"You'll soon want more land and water. When you start spreading out, I'll be there to trim your horns."

"That's where you're wrong, Braggs. I only want the land that's deeded to me. I intend to raise prime bulls for breeding. Hereford cattle are more beefy, more durable, and easier to manage than any other cattle in Montana. You might even decide to mix your herd in a few years."

The news took some of the rancor out of the man's eyes. "Prime Hereford bulls?"

"A good bull is worth a couple of thousand dollars in the right market. Herefords are proving their strength all over the country. Believe me, Braggs, they'll be the beef stock of the future."

"What about Henry's water holes?"

"You must mean the water he acquired by the death of the Bryants." Dave lifted a careless shoulder. "He made no effort to buy the land or water rights. He merely took to using them. I offered to let his cattle water for one cent per head a day. With winter on the way, that wouldn't break him."

Braggs had a different light in his eyes. "Do you think your gunmen can hold off Striker's men? They have you outnumbered three or four to one."

"That's something only time will tell."

Braggs rolled the cigar over from one corner of his mouth to the other. "You've proved that you can handle yourself in a fight, Valeron, but you're no match for me. I have thirty men on my payroll, and Slick Amos had a lot of friends. If you buck me, you're going to get run over."

"Sorry that you feel that way, Braggs. As I told you and Slick, I have no quarrel with the Box Z."

Braggs didn't answer, and quickly melted into the crowd. As the gathering broke up, Dave didn't see him or the Strikers again. He was left with an empty, very alone feeling. He knew what had to be done, but the zest was gone. Colette's mother had been brutally murdered in her bed, and Slick Amos had been buried the day before. Having started, would the fighting ever end?

In spite of Sela Striker's murder, the wedding of Colette and Braggs was still set for the first Saturday in November. It gave Dave precious little time to carry off his plan of action.

Up near the beaver ponds Concho and Short Loop built a cabin for watching the cattle and selling water to Striker should he be forced to bring in his cattle. Pecos stayed at the house, doing the cooking and buying supplies. He approached Dave after breakfast several days after the funeral of Mrs. Striker.

"Storm brewing, son. It looks to be a tough winter ahead."

"I'm surprised that Striker hasn't tried something yet. His cattle must be drying up and blowing away."

"Concho took a ride that way and said that Striker has moved most of his herd onto Box Z range. At the moment, he has Axell on his side and they've combined resources. It makes our chore a bit tougher. I was intending to buck Striker and his crew, but Braggs has a bigger outfit. If we end up battling both of them, we're going to lose, Davy."

"That's the way I figure it too."

"Must have five thousand head of cattle between them, and forty riders or more. We've got four in our number. We never considered odds like those."

"Winter might prevent any real fighting till spring," Dave observed. "Once the snow starts, there'll be no shortage of water."

"Well, no sense in worrying about what might happen. I'm cutting and stacking all of the wood I can. If we get hit with a hard storm, I intend to sit by the fire and keep warm.''

"We ought to put in some extra rations too, in case it gets too cold or dangerous to ride in for supplies.''

Pecos nodded. "What about the wedding tomorrow? You going to attend?''

"I'm going for a ride,'' Dave said, evading an answer. He looked up at the darkening sky. "I hope I don't get caught in the storm that's brewing. I'll be home late or tomorrow morning.''

Pecos smiled. "Don't worry about me, son. I'll be snug and cozy next to the fire.''

Icy-cold blasts bent the tips of the trees, and then they whispered up the canyons like the breath of death itself. The clouds massing over the mountain were black and ominous, forming like a great shroud of impending doom. The birds were strangely silent, and animals that usually scurried in trees or near the beaver ponds were not to be seen.

Dave had seen a number of winters in Montana, but this had been a most unusual season. The drought had been long and hard, burning the grass, drying up the water holes. The autumn had not produced the rains that were usual for the season. Now that a storm was on its way, Dave wondered what they could expect. For the first-of-the-season snows, it was much colder than normal.

Dave turned up his collar, slipped on his buckskin

gloves, and put his horse up the trail through the trees. It was going to be a cold ride.

With eyes that were like fiery pits, the Butcher watched the darkness of the storm gather. With the clouds rolling in low and heavy, it would be an early dusk. That would suit his purpose, for it was Colette's last eve as a single woman. He could not sit back and allow the marriage, not after being so close to eliminating her. He had to kill her this very night, whether he managed to make her suffer or not. It would take only a single thrust of his knife. Even if he were spotted, no one would recognize him under his black hood. He might have laughed at the thought that no one even suspected him, but his mind was suddenly alert.

There in the yard, bundled in a heavy coat, Colette was out trying to take in the frozen wash from the clothesline. It was the ideal situation.

With his natural stealth, the Butcher hurried down the hill, careful not to be seen or heard. He guessed the clothes to be more than the girl could manage in one trip. Once at the base of the hill, he waited until she went into the house with one load. Then he darted across the open yard and to the rear of the tack shed, a position that would put him close enough to strike.

He paused, waiting to attack. His eyes burned with malevolence as he viewed the one dress on the line.

The white gown was not fancy, but it was enough to rip his guts apart. It was a wedding gown!

Colette hurried out of the house once more, and her nimble fingers quickly removed the clothing a piece at a time. She had her back to the Butcher, unaware of his approach until his hand suddenly clapped over her mouth. She struggled, but he was much stronger than she. He dragged her toward the rear of the shed, jerking her violently with each step.

He threw her down and pinned her with one hand. In the other, he drew his large skinning knife.

Dave reached the hollow where he had previously watched the ranch in time to see the Butcher cross the yard. As the black-hooded man took up a hiding place behind the tack shed, Dave started moving toward the house. With Colette inside, he had time to slip down through the brush as well. He was twenty yards from the house when the Butcher grabbed Colette.

Dave broke from the brush and streaked across the open ground toward the two struggling figures. As the man's arm rose to strike with his knife, Dave lunged at him.

The killer heard the footsteps at the last instant, and he turned from his victim and attempted to point the knife at Dave. His actions were a second too late.

The two of them crashed into the shed and fell to

the ground in a tangled heap of arms and legs. Dave feverishly tried to pin the man's knife hand, but the Butcher twisted away and jumped to his feet.

Dave rolled over, came to his knees, and clawed under his coat to free his gun.

Something dug deeply into Dave's shoulder, a searing pain that knocked him back onto his heels. He still managed to get the gun out, but the attacker darted around the shed.

Staggering to his feet, Dave used his left hand to steady the knife that was stuck several inches deep into his shoulder. He tried to run, to cut the man off from his retreat, but he stumbled and fell to his knees. Before he could recover, Colette was at his side, holding him back.

"It's too late, Dave! He's gone!"

Dave groaned from the excruciating pain of the knife wound. It had hit the bone in his shoulder but not anything vital. That much he could assess from the feel and location of the blade.

He groaned louder as he pulled the knife free of his flesh. "Give me something to stop the bleeding. I'm all right."

Colette tore away a piece of her dress and quickly folded it into a wad. After tucking it against the slice in the skin, she wrapped a scarf around his chest to hold it in place. He buttoned down the coat to secure the crude bandage and then he holstered his gun.

"That should hold for a spell," he said. "It's too blasted cold to bleed much."

"What are you doing here? I thought I was dead!"

He grinned at her. "I always seem to be around when that knife-happy maniac comes calling. Saving your life is becoming a habit."

"Let me help you into the house. We'll both freeze out here."

"I'd likely die inside your house, Colette. Henry and his boys would sure like to catch me alone and practically helpless."

She crossed her arms over her chest, shivering from both the cold and the nearness of a violent death. Her thin cotton dress was not much good against the chill of the icy wind, even when wrapped in a mackinaw jacket.

Her teeth were chattering as she spoke again. "W-what now? You ought t-to have some h-help."

Dave could feel the sticky, warmish sensation of blood running down the inside of his shirt, but he would not put his life into Striker's hands. With a considerable effort, he rose to his feet.

"Bring that white dress with you," he said finally. "We're going into town."

"But that's. . . ."

"Do as I say." He cut off her argument. "I saved your life. Now you can save mine."

The wind gusted through the valley, carrying bits of snow. With the bitter cold, the snow did not fall as flakes but as crystals of ice. Dave waited, with his back turned against the storm, his right hand held tightly over his wounded left shoulder.

Colette brought the nearly frozen gown over to him and waited for further orders. He might have smiled at the way she had accepted his authority, but time was too short.

"Let's get to my horse. We can make it to town if we hurry."

"It's going to be a load on one horse," Colette observed.

"He's been getting fat and sassy the past couple of days. A little work won't hurt him."

"Henry will think that I've been kidnapped," Colette said, putting an arm around Dave for support. "You'll end up in jail for taking me with you."

"Maybe . . . maybe not. I made a promise to you that last time I saw you. I always keep my word."

Gathering his strength, Dave turned into the wind and headed toward the distant hill and his mount. If he didn't bleed to death, they would make it to Judge Hammer's place. If he passed out, they might both die on the trail. Colette was shaking from the cold and the snow crystals were coming down harder. He raised his eyes to heaven and made a silent prayer:

Don't let the Butcher strike again while I'm weak and injured. That's all I ask. Don't let him catch us on the trail!

Chapter Ten

Dave felt at the end of his strength, but he remained awake. The doctor finished bandaging the knife wound and then he stepped back to Judge Hammer.

"Another inch toward his heart and the Butcher would have had Colette at his mercy. The bone stopped the blade of the knife, preventing any permanent damage. I'd say that Mr. Valeron was mighty lucky."

"So it would seem," the judge agreed.

Dave straightened in the chair, feeling lightheaded from his loss of blood. His shirt was red-stained from the wound, but the cold had slowed the bleeding considerably.

"I've got a spare shirt in my saddlebags, Judge. We still have something to do . . . remember?"

The old man sighed. "It appears, Doc, that you've been dismissed."

"The young never have much time for gratitude." Doc Taylor grinned. "I'll check on you later in the week," he told Dave. "We can settle your bill then."

"That'll be fine."

Judge Hammer followed the barber and part-time doctor out into the night. He returned with a clean shirt and draped it over the back of a chair near the stove. He had used the same chair to thaw out Colette's dress.

Colette had been warming herself at the fire while the doctor was working on Dave. She seemed subdued and frightened. Dave could only imagine what Jake and Henry would do to her for running off in the night with their hated enemy.

"Taylor will send over Big Ed," Judge Hammer said to Dave. "He'll have a look at the knife and see if anything can be found out about it. Too bad you didn't get a look at the man's face. Mighty hard to find a killer with no identity."

"Three attempts against Colette," Dave said. "I think she must be someone very special to the killer."

"Could be. All the others except Mrs. Striker

were young and single girls. Might also be the fact that she has escaped him and it hurts his pride.''

''It's for sure that he killed Colette's mother by mistake. He was there to kill her and got in the wrong room.''

''That's something to consider in the case, Dave. The men on the Striker ranch would know the right room, so that eliminates them as suspects.''

As he spoke, the judge turned the shirt in front of the fire. He tossed it to Dave and tipped his head toward Colette. ''Did you explain everything yet?''

At Colette's frown, Dave cleared his throat and murmured, ''Not exactly.''

''Think I'll step into the next room for a few minutes. I'll put on some coffee to warm us all up.''

Gingerly, Dave put his left arm through the sleeve of his shirt. Then he managed to get it buttoned. Colette's gaze never wavered from him.

''What devious plan do you have in mind that includes the sheriff and the judge?''

Dave was suddenly unsure of himself. He had rehearsed the words over and over in his head and had reasoned out the logical approach to take. Still, his mind was a total blank.

Colette came over to him. Her eyes searched his face for the answer to her question. Words were not at Dave's bidding, so he rose to his feet and reached out with his good right arm. He encircled her and drew her close. He was warmed at the way she came into his arms. When she kissed him, her delicate lips were soft and eager. It was such a delight that Dave lingered for a long time.

Colette finally pulled back from him. Her complexion was tinted by a pink hue, and she was openly flustered.

"This is not proper, David. After all, I'm supposed to be getting married tomorrow—to another man!"

"I don't think so, Colette," he said. "I believe you're going to get married a little early, and to me."

Her eyes widened in surprise. "But . . . I can't! I mean, how can you . . . ?"

Dave grew serious. "Tell me that you'd rather marry Axell or another man and I'll take you home this minute."

She shook her head sharply, her black, shimmering hair flowing loosely about her face and shoulders.

"But . . . but I have to have consent. I'm not yet twenty-one. Henry has to. . . ."

"That's the part where I come in," the judge spoke up, coming back into the room.

"Anyone ever tell you about eavesdropping, Judge?" Dave asked.

"Never was any good at minding my own business, son. Besides, this is my story."

"What story?" Colette asked. "What are both of you talking about?"

"Your mother came to me a short time after she married Henry. He had been talking about you possibly marrying Tom or Jake when you came of age. She was not altogether pleased with that prospect and asked what could be done.

"To prevent any such idea in the future, we conspired together and told Henry that your name had been legally changed to Striker. That made you his stepdaughter and his sons could never marry you. However, we never actually went through the paperwork, only the preliminaries. Your name is still Colette March and your mother was your only legal guardian."

"But now that she is gone," Colette said, "her death still makes Henry my rightful guardian . . . doesn't it?"

The judge held up a sheet of paper. "She signed this release the day she was killed. I rode out and spoke to her. This is her signed permission for you to marry young Dave."

Colette could not believe her ears. She opened her mouth, but there were no words. Her mother had known that she was going to marry Dave Valeron and not the awful owner of the Box Z!

"I was going to catch you alone and ask you properly," Dave spoke up. "But the Butcher beat me to you and I never got around to it."

"Then . . . then I'm to marry you?" She was still incredulous. "Here? Now? Tonight?"

"It has to be before Henry arrives," the judge warned. "I don't want any confrontation with him except with Big Ed and me. We'll put this to him in words that'll leave no doubt that there's to be no marriage to Axell Braggs."

Dave studied Colette's reaction. It had to be an incredible shock to have all this thrust upon her at one time, and it was a wonder that she didn't scream in confusion and exasperation.

"I'm still asking you, Colette," he told her. "Will you marry me . . . here and now?"

There was a mist in her eyes, but she smiled shyly. "Of course, I'll marry you, David."

He would have let out a whoop of joy, but just then the door opened. It was Big Ed. He closed out the wind and blowing snow, and then removed his hat and shook it.

"Cold night to be out. What's this all about, Judge?"

Colette shrugged out of her coat and took her gown toward the judge's bedroom.

"I won't be a minute."

Ed frowned at seeing the girl in town. "What the . . . ?

"Would you hitch up my horse and carriage, Ed?" Hammer asked. "Dave isn't going to be in very good shape for a hard ride home."

Ed took notice of Dave buttoning his shirt. The bandage was visible enough for him to see it, and he asked, "Where did you get the bum arm, Valeron? Did you cross swords with Henry while you were stealing away his girl?"

"No. It was the Butcher. He was after Colette again."

Ed groaned, stuck his hat back on, and stared hard at Dave. "And I suppose you let him escape?"

"Sorry, Ed. I should have shot him instead of trying to take him alive."

"I spend 'most every night freezing my tail off, watching for him to try something, and you let him get away—twice! I only want one shot at him, one lousy shot. And I won't miss."

"Here's the knife he's been using. Maybe that will help in finding out who he is."

Ed glanced down at it and grunted in disgust. "Only if he was dumb enough to carve his initials in the handle."

As the lawman went out to get the horse and carriage, Judge Hammer took up a vigil at the window.

"This road to revenge, son," he said softly. "Have you considered the effect it'll have on your bride? She's likely to be a widow by spring."

"I couldn't very well let her marry Axell, and there's no reason to believe the Strikers will live longer than I will."

The judge let out a sigh. "That girl has worked like a slave all her life. She has never had a chance at suitors, because Jake drove them all away. Tom and Jake have treated her like dirt, and Henry never took time to show her any of that fatherly love he preaches on Sunday. She's had a miserable life. I would like to see her happy."

"Nothing I'd like better than to make her happy, Judge."

"Once the Strikers know you're Dave Bryant, they might decide you have to be killed. What are you going to do about that?"

"I've told you the steps I've taken against Striker. I have my own cattle, my own land, and my own family and friends to worry about. I was serious about wanting justice for the death of my folks, but it isn't going to ruin the rest of my life."

"Striker might not see it that way."

"I told you that I came to Scofield to ruin and possibly kill the Strikers, Judge. I wanted them to pay the ultimate price for murdering my parents. But there are other things to consider. I've got Concho, Short Loop, Pecos, and now a wife. I won't sacrifice everything for a twelve-year-old vendetta."

"That's well and good, but the Strikers might not believe you're serious."

"If it comes to a fight, I'll win it. I've got too much to live for to let them ruin it this time."

Big Ed came back into the house, stomping the

snow from his boots. He shook off his heavy coat and whistled.

"That stuff is freezing before it hits the ground. Bet we have a foot of ice by morning."

"The storm should keep Striker from coming in till late tomorrow," the judge said. "For one thing, he'll have to make certain that Colette didn't up and run away on her own. By the time he figures that she had help and comes looking, the newlyweds will be safely up at the Bryant place."

Ed groaned. "He'll want their hides then. I hope that someone has a plan to prevent a full-scale war."

Dave spoke up first: "Once Colette is legally married to me, I'll defend my own wife and property, Ed."

"And you and I will speak to Henry personally," the judge said to the sheriff. "The law is on Dave's side this time."

Colette entered before any further conversation. Her hair was still damp from the downpour of ice crystals and snow, but she had managed to comb it out and it cascaded like black, silken threads to caress her face and drape softly onto her shoulders. She didn't have a veil, but in the white gown she looked to Dave like a heavenly vision.

"All the men in the world would surely envy me tonight," he said, awed.

Colette blushed at the flattery and smiled timidly.

"I never even attended a wedding before. I'm afraid I don't know what I'm supposed to do."

Judge Hammer picked up his prayer book and moved to the center of the room. He gave Colette a fatherly smile.

"From this point forward, Colette, I will guide you through it. I've been a justice of the peace for thirty years and never failed to get a bride and groom married properly."

Chapter Eleven

The wind had a bite to it. Dave's fingers and cheeks felt numb from the cold. Bundled beneath the judge's heavy blanket, he used his good hand to direct the horse toward his ranch. The snow gusted in flurries and piled up several inches on the ground. He had to stay alert to the trail or be lost. Even so, he was puzzled by the silence of his new wife. She hadn't spoken a word since they left the judge's house.

As he turned onto a familiar stretch of road, he took a moment to glance at her. She was huddled close to him for warmth, but she didn't lock her arm around his. In fact, she seemed to avoid looking in his direction.

"What's the matter, Colette?" he asked, growing tired of the strained silence.

She tossed her head in a negative shake, and then stared at the dark trail ahead.

"Come on, something has put a burr under your saddle. What is it?"

As she glanced at him, there was no love or devotion in her expression. Instead, she appeared angry.

"I thought my name would be Mrs. David Valeron. It was something of a shock to hear myself being pronounced Mrs. Bryant! I can see now why you showed so much interest in me."

He stared at her blankly. "I don't see what you're getting at."

"Don't you?" Her voice was full of sarcasm.

"No. I took an interest in you before I even knew who you were. Learning that you were a Striker, I was at a loss as to what to do."

"I didn't fit into your plans for revenge. Is that it?"

He hated the tone of her voice. It was obvious that she felt he had used her for his petty revenge. How could he convince her that he was serious?

"You have nothing to do with my vengeance against the Strikers."

"Oh no? What could be better than this little stunt? You take me right out of their yard and whisk me away. They spend all night searching and finally discover that I'm married to a man they hate. I'd say that you managed to find a degree of satisfaction in that."

Dave pulled the horse to a stop and sat there in silence. He tried to sort out some kind of logic to demonstrate that his intentions were strictly honorable.

"I did return to Scofield for revenge," he admitted. "I knew that the Lazy S had to have our water to survive a long drought. My father had known as much, so he let Henry run his cattle on our upper range in exchange for a share of his herd. When he changed his mind one season, Henry killed both my father and my mother. Pecos Thorn, our only hired man at the time, took me with him and escaped to Wyoming.

"For twelve years I've worked with a single goal in mind: I wanted justice for the murder of my parents. Pecos had the deed to the ranch, and we kept the taxes paid while I grew older and earned enough to start a new herd. Striker was never smart enough to try to buy the land. I set out to ruin him."

"And you'll do it unless he kills you," Colette said. "But your story is a little different from the one I heard. There was an argument between your father and Henry. Sam Bryant was supposed to have killed your mother, and Henry shot and killed Sam afterward."

That jolted Dave. "The sheriff said the deaths

were blamed on Indians, and now Striker says that my father killed my mother. Three stories and no real answers. Who told you that version?''

''A man I trust,'' she said. ''He wouldn't have lied to me about it.''

Dave decided that he would have a few words with Pecos about that. Surely, the man who had raised him all those years knew most of the facts surrounding his parents' deaths. After all, he was there at the time. He had told Dave that Striker was responsible for both deaths. That was good enough for him.

''The storm's getting worse,'' Colette remarked, as if prompting him to resume their journey.

Dave held the reins tight in his good hand. He took a deep breath and turned toward Colette.

''That's a good horse strapped into harness, Mrs. Bryant. The judge will be real upset if something happens to him. He has worked up a sweat pulling us through the snow. If I make him stand there long enough, he'll freeze in his tracks.''

''Then why are—''

''But,'' he cut her off, ''I'm not going to have you thinking poorly of me on our first night together. If you want to think that I'm here only to get revenge on the Strikers, that's fine. If you want to think that I'm a pigheaded jackass, that's fine too. In fact, I don't care what else you think about me, but I won't have you thinking that I married you for spite.''

He could see her eyes brightly glowing as she tried to assess his sincerity. And so he pressed his slight advancement in her esteem.

"I would have married you tonight no matter whose daughter you were, and I'll darn well fight any man who tries to take you away from me. I didn't fall in love with you as a part of my plan for revenge. I fell in love with you because you are a beautiful, sweet, and very special lady."

"You can't love someone you hardly know," she protested.

"Why did you let me kiss you, and more than once?"

She grew flustered and ducked her head. "I . . . that was. . . ." She moistened her lips. "I owed you my life. I felt that I had to repay you in . . . in some way."

"You're not that kind of woman," he said decisively. "I wouldn't have fallen in love with a woman who repaid her debts with her favors."

"I don't have to explain my actions to you. You were using me to get back at—"

He cut off her argument by kissing her soundly. Her lips were tentative at first, but Dave willed her to accept him. His was a love message that could not be misunderstood. When he pulled away, he found that Colette was completely out of breath.

"We'll freeze to death along with the horse if we don't get started for home, Mrs. Bryant. I love you because you're you. I can't put it into any plainer words than that.''

Slowly, the whisper of a smile spread along her lips. ''Sparking under the pale moonlight is one thing, David, but this is hardly the time or place for romance.'' The smile grew until her teeth sparkled. ''Why don't you take me home?''

Axell Braggs attracted no particular attention, as he sat alone in the rear of the Red Moose Saloon. He had been in town for several hours before Striker and his two sons came trudging in out of the foot-deep snow. Even as he looked them over, he knew that the rumor was true—Colette had married Dave Valeron.

Jake and Tom swung over to the bar to order drinks. Only Henry himself came back to join Axell. He jerked out a chair and plopped down dejectedly.

''Can you believe them lying females?'' Henry snapped. ''Married to a woman for eight years and she lies to me about changing Colette's name to Striker!''

''It would seem that you've lost some of your bargaining power, Henry. I don't intend to wage war with Valeron for my own injured pride within the community.''

''That ain't the half of it, Axell. Dave's real last name is Bryant.''

Braggs didn't even blink. ''That comes as no real

surprise. I was always puzzled that a stranger would move in and try to ruin you.''

Henry looked at Braggs expectantly. ''What would it take for you to put an end to Dave Bryant?''

''Why me? What's the matter with your own men?''

''I can't order the death of a man, Axell. I'm leader of the Sunday prayer meetings. I've got to set an example.''

Axell laughed without humor. ''You're a sorry individual. 'Pious,' 'sanctimonious,' 'hypocrite'— do those words have a meaning to you?''

Henry ignored his barbs. ''There's a point that I won't go beyond. I killed a man once and it has haunted me ever since. I can't define it, but I know that I'll never take up a gun against another man again.''

''If this snow keeps coming, your herd is going to be in deep trouble. The stuff is caked into ice when it hits the ground. I wonder if any of our cattle will survive.''

''What are your terms, Axell? You wouldn't have come to this meeting if you weren't willing to make a deal.''

''I have a couple of men who would like a shot at Bryant. Slick Amos had some friends, but I've held them back.''

''Why?''

He lifted a careless shoulder. ''I wanted to see

what would happen. This Bryant character has some grit, Henry. I've been watching him build up his place. I've seen those new cattle of his. Very impressive property he's making for himself.''

''What are your terms?'' Henry asked again. ''Name them.''

Axell fingered the scar on his chin thoughtfully. ''First, I get half of your cattle but in the spring, not right now. I don't want a bunch of extra corpses littering my pastures.''

Henry gulped down that suggestion. ''Half of my remaining herd?''

''Second, I want you to do nothing with Mrs. Bryant. When the time comes, I'll tend to her personally.''

''She'll never marry you,'' Henry pointed out. ''She has no reason to do what anyone tells her any longer. She has Dave Bryant's name.''

''Like I said, you leave her entirely alone. When she's all by herself in the world, without a dime to her name, without anyone to turn to, she might be less trouble to manage than you think.''

''That part is no problem, but half of my herd is too high a price.''

''You offered me five hundred head before. How many of your cattle will be lost to the winter kill?''

Henry sighed. He was beaten and miserable. ''All right, Axell. I'll abide by your terms. When will you take care of Bryant?''

''You won't have a long wait, but I want it to look like an accident. No need to have Ed pointing the finger of suspicion at either of us.''

Feeling much older than his age, Henry rose from the table. A few drinks might make the trip back home a mite warmer and remove the bad taste from his mouth. Once the storm broke, they would have to move their herd back onto their own winter range. There was still a little grass, but it was buried under the snow. With luck, the storm would break and melt off.

Dave had never felt more satisfied with life. He tested his arm and discovered some pain, but it worked. Pecos was sticking wood into the fire as Colette cleared away the breakfast dishes.

''Smart man you are, Davy,'' Pecos said with a wide grin. ''That gal is a dandy cook. I'm already looking forward to supper.''

''Better be looking forward to moving the cattle around some today. If it doesn't warm up, we'll have to keep them from bunching too tightly.''

''Wish we had a shelter for them. Be a real shame to have a herd of only a hundred and have them all die.''

''With four of us, that's only twenty-five head of cattle apiece. We could practically house them inside the two cabins.''

"Not if I have to clean house," Colette chirped from the kitchen sink.

"I'll get my horse," Pecos said with a laugh. "I wouldn't want to wind up on the outside looking in for the evening meal."

"Best snag one for me too. I want to look over the canyon and see if we ought to push them higher."

"Sure that you're up to it?"

"I'm fine, Pecos. Too much to do around here to sit by the fire."

As Pecos went out into the cold morning air, Colette came in, wiping her hands on a makeshift apron.

"Need to round you up some things," Dave told her. "You're wearing a flour sack for an apron and have only a wedding gown and a torn housedress to wear. I think we'll schedule a trip into town first thing and get you a wardrobe."

She smiled warmly and sat down on his lap. She was careful not to put any pressure on his left shoulder as she put her arms about his neck and kissed him.

"Am I to be a spoiled wife?"

"Pampered as much as possible," he replied. "Whatever your heart desires, I'll do my best to see that you get it."

"Then stay home today. You lost a lot of blood last night, and no telling where that Butcher is. I need my husband here at home to protect me."

"There isn't anything in the world I'd rather do,

but those cattle are our future. If they die, I'm broke. How'd you like to be married to a typewriter sales-man, a man who spends eight to ten months traveling away from home each year?''

"No, thanks." She kissed him lightly again, a sort of good-bye peck. As she stood up, she used a motherly tone of voice: "Out into the cold with you, David. Can't have you being in the way while I'm trying to do my housework."

He picked up his coat, but stopped at the door and said, "Should Henry stop by, tell him I've de-cided to let him water his cattle for nothing. He will have to use the upper ponds, because I'll still keep the lower ones fenced for our herd." He sighed. "Revenge or justice—it isn't worth the chance of losing you."

Colette's eyes misted. "I'm sorry I ever thought that you might have married me for spite, David. Can you forgive me?"

"I'll let you make it up to me a little at a time. Thirty or forty years ought to do it."

She smiled and he went out into the cold. He felt much better for relenting in his vows of revenge. Pecos and the boys needed a home. So did he. No need risking any more lives on something that hap-pened twelve long years ago.

Chapter Twelve

Dave and Pecos circled the upper range and found that all the cattle were bunched up in the canyon. It was protected by walls from some of the bitter wind. The snow was drifting in many places, some of it three feet deep, and it was still coming down, a light and steady snowfall.

"Looks as if the boys are down in the canyon," Pecos said, nodding toward two distant riders.

"They'll make certain that the herd keeps moving tonight. I don't envy either of them on that shift."

"They're good men, Davy. We were lucky to find them both."

"I only hope these Herefords are all you told me

129

they were, Pecos. Otherwise, we'll be out of business before this storm is over.''

"If we lose this herd, there won't be another cow standing, either. Then these beef can live off tree bark or sagebrush if need be, and they're smarter than regular cows. They don't blunder into a storm— they turn their backs to it and stay together for warmth. They'll make it all right.''

Dave appraised the old man. He was white haired, with leathery skin, flinty eyes, and as tough as a sun-parched boot. He was thin with age, his shoulders bowed from too many hours in the saddle, but he was a smart, hearty wrangler. Dave could not recall Pecos's looking any older from one year to the next. He was personable, easygoing, and had never uttered a word of complaint in raising Dave to manhood. All told, he was as near a father as Dave had ever known.

"I've listened to a story that's told hereabouts," he said casually to Pecos. "Word has it that Sam Bryant killed his wife." He watched the man's reaction. "That story goes that Henry killed Sam after Mary was already dead.''

Pecos didn't meet Dave's probing stare. That was significant in itself. "And who done told you that, Davy?''

"Doesn't really matter," he evaded carefully. "But it set me to wondering about my parents' deaths.''

"Yeah?"

"You never did say that Henry Striker actually murdered both of my folks. I've believed it, for I watched him kill my father. Now I'm wondering about my mother's death."

"There ain't nothing to be done about any of it now. You'll get revenge on Striker by cutting off his water. He'll be ruined by midsummer of next year."

"I've decided to let him have access to our water, Pecos."

That startled the man. "You what?"

Dave lifted his shoulders to shake the snow from his heavy coat. He winced at the pain that shot through his injured shoulder. "I'm not going to risk losing a woman like Colette or getting one of you men killed over some ancient vendetta. If I was sure that Henry had killed both of my parents, I might still want justice. After what I've heard, I'm not sure any longer what is right."

"Are you going soft now that you're a married man?"

"Could be. I've a lot to lose now. If it came to a war, I would probably kill the Strikers and maybe end up in prison for a time."

"We've discussed that possibility over the years. You used to think it was worth the risk."

"Maybe not," Dave said. "I witnessed Henry shoot and kill my father. I know that my father was shouting and cussing, but he didn't have a gun. That was a cold-blooded killing. I didn't see how my mother was killed.'' He put a hard look on Pecos. ''Want to tell me the whole story?''

Pecos suddenly appeared his age. There was a hollow expression in his eyes, as if a burden he packed had become too great a weight to carry.

''Maybe I've been wrong to nurse your hate all these years, Davy. I thought it would make a better man out of you. It has worked to a degree. Look at what you've managed in your young life—a herd of prime Hereford cattle, a place of your own, a pretty wife, and a crew working for you.

''When we lit out that first night, you were just a frightened kid. You wanted to run and hide. I never wanted you to be a sissy, and so I helped you find a reason to be strong. You're everything I could have wanted in a son, Davy. I've been afraid at times that the bitterness and hate would destroy you, but you've become a man. Now that you've decided to forget your revenge, your education and maturity are complete. You've become more of a man than I've ever been. I'm right proud of that.''

''Then what's the real truth about my mother's death? Was it my father who killed her?''

''Striker was unhappy that your dad was asking so much for his water rights. They argued and it about come to blows. Your mother got between them, trying to calm them both. Sam was out of control. You certainly remember him as having a temper. Well, Henry was of the same mold.

"Anyhow, Sam throwed your ma out of the way. She fell and hit her head on the foot of the stove. It cracked her skull and she died a few minutes later. Both Henry and Sam were with her when she breathed her last.

"Henry roared that it had been Sam's fault for pushing Mary. Sam yelled back that Henry had caused her death by not accepting the terms of their agreement. Sam grabbed a poker and took after Henry. He might have killed him, but Henry got to his horse, yanked out his rifle, and shot Sam dead." Pecos took a breath. "That's the part that you heard and saw—the yelling and the shooting in the yard. It's true that Sam was unarmed, but he was intent on killing Henry. A jury might even have considered his actions as self-defense."

After a long pause, Dave spoke quietly. "It's over then, Pecos. I'll ride over and tell Striker that they're free to use the water and with no conditions. They can lend us some manpower next spring to help us build better dams and put a fence up to keep their cattle on their own side."

"Maybe I should come along. Striker might be in a foul mood after your taking Colette like you did."

"I'll handle it myself. I'll be back before dark."

"See that you are," Pecos advised. "Not only is

this snow beginning to pile up, but that new bride of yours will be pacing like a caged animal while she waits for you.''

Dave grinned. ''You don't have to tell me twice to hurry.''

He headed his horse into the trees, picking out the trail he had used on his previous trips to the Lazy S. It wound along the crest of the mountain rim and skirted two deep canyons.

Dave contemplated what he had learned from Pecos. It all made sense now, and Striker was not so much to blame as he had thought. He remembered seeing his father shot down. The man could have had a poker in his hand at the time. It had happened so suddenly, and had been a shock to his system.

He took a deep breath and let it out. There was a great relief, like the removal of a pile of rocks from his shoulders. It was all over. There would be no war, no fighting.

Dave allowed his horse to pick its way along the steep precipice that divided two separate buttes. It was the only narrow and dangerous part of the journey. Once past the twin canyons, the mountainous range spilled steadily downward to the valley where the Strikers had built their ranch.

His mount slowed, cautiously stepping over a downed log, remaining a full four or five feet from the edge of the crevice. Dave considered them past danger when his horse suddenly jerked backward.

At the same time, a shot echoed through the mountains.

Dave tried to roll free of the saddle, but the horse's action had been instinctive, without warning, and he could not fight free of the heavy coat or the stirrups. The horse went to its knees, then pitched right over the edge of the cliff, taking Dave with it.

Axell Braggs looked over the barrel of his smoking rifle. He felt no real satisfaction in killing a man he hardly knew. Dave Valeron or Bryant—it made no difference to him. He had taken away the girl who was to have been his own wife, but he didn't hold that against the man. Colette would be his soon enough, now that the interloper was out of the way.

Sticking the rifle back into the boot, he wondered if anyone had heard the shot. He decided that it was highly unlikely, for the cold wind was gusting through the trees and the falling snow deadened all sounds. If the fall into the canyon didn't kill Bryant, the snow and cold certainly would. There were more black clouds rolling into the valley and the temperature was dropping with each passing minute. There was no chance that the man could survive. Better yet, it would look like an accident. No one would point a finger at him.

Axell resisted the urge to ride over and look down into the jagged crevice. If someone did happen along, he didn't wish to leave any tracks. He'd hit the horse behind the ear, where no one would be likely to find a bullet hole. It would appear that the animal slipped and the two of them fell to their deaths.

The snow increased in density as Axell made his way up the side of the mountain. He circled toward the Striker place, picked up the trail of several cattle, and mixed in his tracks. With the heavy snow, there would be no way to follow him. He had done the job to perfection.

He smiled broadly. It had been his good fortune to witness Bryant and one of his riders split up. Once Axell guessed Bryant's direction, he had been able to cut him off and set his trap.

He felt some curiosity as to why Bryant was heading toward the Striker place, but that was one answer he would never know. Maybe he had been going over to set the record straight about his marrying Colette. He might have wanted to blackmail Henry for more money to water his cattle. It didn't matter anymore. Dave Bryant would not be heard from again.

Dave licked the ice from his lips and strained to get his face out of the snow. His left arm didn't work, and he hurt from his toenails to his hat, which was still bound onto his head by his scarf. He grunted and finally got his good right arm under his chest.

With a great deal of effort, he lifted himself high enough to take a look around.

The walls of the crevice rose straight up in front of him. Covered with ice and snow, they were broken only by a few hearty shrubs and jagged rocks. The ground under Dave was the base floor between the two canyon faces and located in a run-off gully that led down into the valley. It was steep, rocky, and had a number of sheer, smooth cliff formations along its path. The wash itself was twenty feet deep, sided by slippery sandstone and granite. It would be impossible to climb out of such a high-walled trench.

Dave tried to flex the fingers on his right hand and he found them completely numb. He removed his glove with his teeth and shoved his hand into his coat and under his armpit. His legs were battered from the fall, but he had landed on his horse's body, which had probably saved his life. He was bruised and battered but in one piece.

Each deep breath hurt his ribs, and his left arm was certainly broken. Other than that, he could still move about. The problem was, what to do next?

He pulled his slightly warmed hand out of his shirt and placed it over one ear and then the other to remove the frost. He was uncertain how long he had been unconscious, but there was no frostbite—yet.

Tucking his knees under him, Dave struggled to an upright position and rocked back onto his heels. The action sent searing spasms through his chest and entire left side. He held on to the pain, using it to combat the numbing cold.

The horse was lying in a grotesque position, with its head twisted backward under its body pointing in the wrong direction. His rifle was smashed and pinned beneath the horse. He had no tools, no food, not even a rope.

There might have been a chance to signal someone if he had both matches and some dry wood. The trouble was, Pecos and the others wouldn't be concerned about his absence until it was fully dark, and he could easily freeze to death before they even started looking. Besides that, he was deep in the notch in the canyon. A man would have to be standing right at the rim to see any signal fire.

Dave did have his handgun, so he could fire off a couple of shots every once in a while and hope someone heard him. Other than that, he was on his own to keep from dying of exposure.

Making the only sensible decision, he took hold of a jagged rock and slowly dragged himself up to his feet. He swayed back and forth for a time, testing for any other injuries. He discovered nothing that would stop him from walking. He had to bend slightly to take a deep breath, and he could feel the wetness of blood on his right knee. Other than the scratches and his broken arm, which he was able to secure inside his coat, he figured that he had been darned lucky to survive.

Several times, he scrutinized the top of the canyon rims. It was odd that whoever had shot his horse and knocked both of them into the canyon didn't check to see that the job was done properly. Of course, looking at the black sky, feeling the constant drop in temperature, and treading two feet of snow in the low spots, the man had been almost certain. It would take even a healthy man several hours to get out of that hole in the summertime. Here Dave was shattered from the fall and already suffering from a knife wound. With a ground blizzard moving in and below-zero temperatures, his death was practically a certainty.

Dave took two steps, then slipped and went to his knees. It jolted him throughout and brought a gasp to his lips. He blinked at a trail of blood that came from somewhere on his head. A less determined man would have sat down, gone to sleep, and given up the ghost. The odds were all against him. He had virtually no chance for survival.

But Dave closed his eyes and pictured Colette in his mind. He clung to the image and drew his strength from it. After a few seconds to recover from the waves of agonizing pain, he was straining to get onto his feet once more. He blindly staggered forward, taking the only route open to him. There was a sheer drop-off that formed the first of many treacherous falls and impossible cliffs and craters. He had no idea how he would get down each of them, but he would not sit around and die. Whoever had tried to kill him would have to do better than that. If he wanted Dave Bryant's hide, he would darn well have to earn it first.

Chapter Thirteen

Colette stood on the porch of the three-room house. With her arms wrapped tightly around her, she peered into the cold wind and icy pellets of snow. She took the lantern from the house and hung it on the porch, hoping that the beacon might guide David back to her.

"You can't stand out here in this blizzard," Pecos said from behind her. "You'll catch your death."

"He should have been back before now. You know he should have been back."

"Come inside," he urged, gently tugging her sleeve. "I'll get bundled up and go look for him, but you got to promise to keep the door bolted and stay in the house. That killer has stalked you two or three times, and Dave would skin me alive if something happened to you.''

Colette backed into the house and closed the door. She watched as Pecos put on his jacket and then his heavy coat. He wrapped his ears with a long scarf and put on two pairs of gloves.

''I hate to have you go out in this,'' she apologized.

The old man grinned. ''I've been pacing the floor too, young lady. I can't sit around the stove while he might be out there afoot.''

''What could have happened to him?''

''The snow is belly deep to a horse, and I'd expect that his mount has worn himself out. I'll take a second animal along, just in case.''

''It's black as the bottom of a well, Pecos. What good can you do alone?''

''I'll round up the boys. With three of us looking, we can cover a lot of territory. Each of us will carry a lantern. Dave is smart enough to hole up for the night if he can't get back home. He's a bright one, that boy.''

Colette watched him go and then bolted the door behind him. She loaded the shotgun and placed it next to the door, but there was little chance that the Butcher would be out in this storm.

She paced the floor and wrung her hands. Never in her life had she felt such worry for anyone. Coming into her life like a breath of fresh air, Dave had whisked her along at his side. He had swept her off her feet and into his heart, and she had made the trip willingly, even eagerly and without reservation. She had never known the love of a man, never really cared to be near one before. Men had always looked, acted, and sounded like the Striker boys—coarse, hard, cruel. Dave had shattered her conception of men, showing her compassion and tenderness. It was something she wanted desperately to keep.

"Please, God," she whispered reverently, staring through the fogged window, "please bring him back to me."

Dave blindly staggered into the wall of the gully. The force of hitting the solid object knocked him to the ground. He lay on the soft cushion of snow and drew in great gulps of air.

His chest was afire from his efforts, and he felt the twinge from his cracked or broken ribs with every breath. His legs were scraped and bleeding, and his body was bruised and battered from the abuse it had suffered. His head spun, making it impossible to focus his eyes, and he had to feel his way along the perilous, narrow gorge. He could not begin to count the number of times he had fallen, slipped, or tumbled down headfirst. He had landed hard enough to knock himself senseless several times, and yet he was still fighting, resolutely clawing his way toward the mouth of the canyon. Once he reached the trail, it was only two or three miles to his house. He could make it. He had to! He had to!

With a renewed effort, Dave turned over and got his legs under him. He fought against the waves of dizziness and pain, and finally dragged himself up to his feet. He had to keep moving, for he had worked up a sweat. To stop was to die. Idle for ten or fifteen minutes, he would freeze to death.

He peered through the swirling snow and got his bearings. The wash didn't seem as deep as before. The ravine was beginning to fade back to smaller hills. It was too dark to see more than shadows, but he had a feeling he had made good progress. He gritted his teeth and bowed his shoulders against the storm.

I'm coming, Colette, he repeated time and again. "I'm coming!" he growled aloud. "No one is going to stop me from having a life with you. I'll kill anyone who tries to come between us!"

The anger drove him, but the sound was as hollow as his waning strength. He was on the verge of defeat. If he didn't reach the road soon, he might not make it.

No bellyaching, Bryant! You ain't quitting! The trail can't be much farther!

Concho greeted Pecos and informed him that Short Loop was up with the cattle. He listened as

Pecos told him about Dave's not returning from his trip to the Strikers.

"You think they bushwhacked him?"

"I don't know, Concho. I'm going to ride the trail and see what I can find."

"You'd better take the lower route, Pecos. I'll pick a good horse and go the short way over the hills. No offense, but that's a hard trail even with the light of day."

Pecos narrowed his brows. "You going to spout something about me being too old to manage it?"

"Gold in your teeth, silver in your hair, and lead in your breeches, old-timer. I'd say that you've not only passed your prime but you've done knocked it flat and stomped on it a time or two."

Pecos tugged at the wrap around his ears. Then he smashed his hat down harder on his head. "Come one of these days, I'm going to pin your ears back, you big-talking coyote. I'll show you just how the cow ate the cabbage."

Concho laughed. "Don't be letting your mouth make bets that your body can't back up, Pecos. You take the lower route. I'll be heading out in five minutes."

"You're like a river, Concho—small at the head and big at the mouth. Soon as we have time, I'll teach you the manners that your ma neglected to learn you."

"Not tonight, old-timer. Let's get out into the cold

and stir up some snow. If Dave is down, he'll need help right pronto.''

Pecos went back to his horse. He set himself in the saddle and wrapped his poncho around his body for protection from the snow and wind. He hooked the lamp over the horn of the saddle and started along the invisible trail.

It was impossible going, fighting three feet of snow, the blowing ice pellets, and bone-penetrating wind that cut through a man's coat like a razor. But Pecos was a Montanan, born to hard winters and experienced from years in the saddle. He slipped the scarf around his face, leaving only his eyes free to search the dim outline of the white, gloomy world around him. His horse was a tough animal, long of hair and thick of hide. He plunged through the drifts and broke his own trail like a good lead steer.

The road was discernible only from the width of the path that showed no growth of brush protruding. Pecos rode for a solid hour without any sign of life. He kept his eyes moving and blinked constantly against the sting of the frozen crystals of snow. It was a fool's errand, trying to find a man in the middle of a blizzard. He could see only eight to ten feet in front of the horse. How could he ever hope to find. . . .

Pecos came erect as he noticed that his horse had suddenly perked his ears toward something on the trail ahead. There was a dark form there, out of place in the middle of the trail. It might be an animal, a bear, or a coyote.

"Dave!" he called, barely getting the word out through his wrapped face.

It was a queer world of pain and unconsciousness to Dave, lost in a limbo at times, then suffering from the incredible agony that came from warming his near-frozen body. He was vaguely aware of someone's tender touch, of treatments to thaw the cold from his feet and hands, of bandages being tightly wrapped around his ribs and legs. He knew that he was back at the ranch, although he was uncertain how far he had made it on his own.

The hours seemed endless, torn between dreams and a half consciousness that allowed him to hear Colette's voice at times. He seemed to sleep for days before his mind was willing to allow him full access to his faculties. When he finally managed to pry open the windows to his eyes, he found himself in darkness.

"Are you all right?" Colette's voice was soft, her murmur like the whisper of a gentle breeze. "Do you need anything?"

Dave did not have the strength to turn his head to look at her. "I . . . I told you that I'd be back," he managed to whisper hoarsely.

There was a movement and then pressure on the

bed next to him. A face appeared above his own, full of concern and worry, but very lovely.

"I never doubted your word for a moment," she said in a hushed voice. Tears were visible in her eyes, and her features were incredibly soft in the dim light.

"You're a beautiful woman, Mrs. Bryant," he whispered.

Colette kissed him lightly and lay down at his side. She cradled him in her arms, and he found it wonderfully reassuring.

"Get some rest, darling. I'm here with you."

Dave relaxed in the delicious warmth of her embrace. When Colette spoke again, her voice was too distant to hear clearly. He should have been refreshed from so many hours in bed, but he was tired . . . so tired. . . .

Henry placed his hands on his hips and twisted his face in anger. He glared at Pecos and met him squarely, poised as if the two of them were about to do combat.

"I'm telling you straight, Pecos. Not one of my men has been off the place in the past two days. We've been fighting this ice storm. If Bryant got himself hurt, it wasn't our doing."

"It took some looking, but I found the slug in his horse, Striker. Want to tell me who else wants that boy dead besides you?"

Henry shook his head. "How should I know? I ought to have come riding over and broken every bone in his body. We spent most of the night looking for Colette. We figured that that sleazy Butcher had done stole her away and maybe killed her!"

"He would have too, but Dave arrived in time to save her neck. You don't guard your place worth a pinch of salt. If you'd been alert, you'd have caught that scum when he killed your wife."

Henry's face grew dark and stormy. "Don't put the blame of my dead wife on my head. By heaven, I won't stand here and put up with that!"

Pecos straightened, but felt the stiffness in his back from the long ride. He held up a hand as a gesture of peace, and then he arched his back and groaned.

"Fighting is for younger men than us two, Striker. I didn't come here to start swinging fists or firing my gun."

Henry also simmered down. He went to the stove and took off the big pot of coffee. He poured himself a cup and then one for Pecos.

"As God is my witness, Pecos, no one from this ranch has lifted a hand against Dave Bryant. I lead the Sunday prayer meetings, and so I've got to set an example. I'll never take up arms to kill another man."

"You mean the way you done Davy's pa?"

That hit Henry hard. He took a sip of coffee and

stared into the cup. A distant look entered his expression. When he answered, it was a tired, weary, and beaten man who spoke.

"That's exactly what I mean, Pecos. I relive that day in my mind every night. I should have run from him, but I didn't. He killed his wife with that temper of his, and I killed him with my own temper. I've never let myself lose my temper like that again."

"Maybe not, but you let Jake run around like an animal. He has bullied everyone in the valley, including Davy's wife."

"This place will be his one day. I've let him take the reins and handle the problems concerning the ranch. He's a bit headstrong, but he'll come around."

"All right, Striker. I didn't come here to start a feud. I'm taking your word that Davy never got this far. If he had, you would have had no reason to ambush him."

"Why's that?"

"He's going to let you have the water you need, and with no fee or charge whatsoever."

Henry frowned. "Why the change of heart?"

"Davy's a married man now. He wants to get along with his neighbors and let the ghosts of the past remain buried."

"You don't say?" Henry was dumbfounded.

"The land will still be fenced, but your cattle will be able to water at the upper ponds. We might even put in a dam come summer to help keep a better supply.''

''Bryant must be scared of us to make such an offer.''

Pecos narrowed his gaze. ''He's trying to do the right thing, Striker. If you leave him alone, he'll forget the differences of our past. If you want to fight him—well, you've seen what he did to Jake and Slick Amos.''

''We'll see what comes about. Jake is not apt to forget the beating he took, but I might be able to hold him back.''

''If he's got any common sense, he'll darn well want to settle this peacefully. We're not looking for any trouble, but we sure won't back away from it, either.''

Henry took a sip of coffee and nodded to the cup Pecos held. ''Finish your belly-warmer and ride out, because Jake will be back anytime. I'll speak to him about this here newfound friendship of ours.''

Pecos set down the cup. ''You do that, Striker. Call him off if you want peace in this valley. Let him come if you want him dead and buried.''

Chapter Fourteen

The snow continued to fall through most of November and into December. Then a break in the weather offered sunshine and the first warm spell that Montana had seen in a long time. Hope sprang up that the melting snow would allow the cattle to dig out some of the sparse vegetation below it, but it was a short-lived hope. Instead of helping the cattle, the temperature dropped once more, freezing a crust on the snow.

Cattle rubbed their noses raw trying to penetrate the icy thickness. They survived on tree bark and twigs from protruding shrubbery. Then, on January ninth, sixteen more inches of snow fell, blanketing all of Montana in a white shroud of death. When the thermometer registered forty-six degrees below zero, the cattlemen called an emergency meeting in Scofield.

Dave and Pecos represented their ranch, with two neighboring cattlemen from the next county being the only ones besides the Lazy S and Box Z to attend.

Big Ed sat next to the room's only stove. He held a telegram, one of the few messages to get through in over a month.

The three Strikers sat together on one side, with Axell Braggs and three of his men on the other. The Judge was also in attendance, as was Doc Taylor.

"I summoned you fellows together at your own request," Ed began. "This is an informal meeting, so speak up when you have a mind. Today is the fifteenth day of January, and we've suffered nearly forty below for six nights in a row, with no break in sight. Things are desperate."

"What about the telegram?" Braggs asked. "Can we get any help from the Army?"

"Word from the Army is that this here storm has laid waste all of the country between the Canadian border and Texas. They have pleas from every corner of the state for emergency feed for cattle, but they simply don't have it to give."

"Let's face it," Dave spoke up. "We should all have stocked up on feed for the winter. We weren't prepared for this kind of weather."

"If the weather doesn't break soon, every cow in

the country will die,'' Axell said solemnly. ''What can we do to prevent that from happening?''

''I took inventory in town,'' Doc Taylor said. ''There's barely enough grain to keep the horses from starving. There isn't any freight moving anywhere in the country. We're getting short of food and supplies because all trade routes are socked in. It'll be weeks before anyone can move a wagon.''

Ed shook his shaggy head. ''I've word that six people here in Bear County have died from the cold, and the Army has reported that hundreds have already perished from the cold within the state. This is the worst winter Montana has ever seen. It's tough to get people worrying over cattle when they're freezing to death themselves.''

''I knew this meeting would be a waste of time,'' Jake Striker snorted. ''We rode through five miles of ice in forty-below weather to cry on each other's shoulders.'' He rose to his feet. ''Well, crying ain't going to save our cattle. We've counted near five hundred dead already. They're piled up in some of the coves where they gathered to get out of the wind. Come spring, there'll be the stink of dead meat for miles around.''

''How about *your* herd, Braggs?'' Judge Hammer asked. ''How many have you lost?''

''Less than Striker, but my cattle were in better shape. We've given them ample water and pretty good feed throughout the fall. His cows had to crowd onto my range for a time before the storm hit.''

''Thanks to you, Bryant!'' Jake glared hard at Dave. ''You helped destroy a big share of our herd!''

''If you'll think back,'' Pecos took up for Dave, ''over a hundred head of the cattle belonged to Davy's pa ten years back. You took them and his water to increase your own herd. You've got no gripe against us!''

Henry held back Jake as he poised to wade in with fists swinging. Big Ed also moved in between the Strikers and Dave and Pecos.

''There'll be no trouble, boys,'' Ed ordered. ''We're here to see what can be done about saving your herds.''

''It's a waste of time,'' Henry said. ''There ain't nothing to do but try to keep the cattle from bunching up and smothering one another. We're heading home.''

The icy wind whistled through the open door and chilled the room as the Strikers went back out into the cold. The judge closed it quickly behind them, rubbed his hands together, and stepped over to warm himself at the stove. ''Any way to move the cattle into the protection of one of the canyons?'' he asked.

''That only encourages them to bunch up,'' Axell replied. ''Like Henry said, we're losing as many from suffocation as from freezing and lack of food.''

"How about your herd, Dave? How is that new breed holding up?"

"We're keeping them in the shelter of the upper canyon. We have one rider out to keep them moving. So far, we've only lost four."

"Good ratio compared to the other herds," Ed said. "Maybe them Herefords are smarter than regular cattle after all."

As Axell stood up, his men did the same. He said, "I rode in to see if the Army had some way to get some winter feed to us. I don't see that there's anything else to gain at this meeting."

"Thanks for coming," Judge Hammer told him. "Looks as if our only hope is that the weather breaks."

The other visiting ranchers also bundled up in their coats and left. Facing the loss of their entire herds, they were a glum group. Before Dave and Pecos could leave, Ed stopped them.

"How're you mending up, Bryant?"

Dave flexed his tender left arm. "I'm getting some use back. The bone set and healed real good. Doc says it'll take time to regain the strength, so I'm careful not to strain myself. The ribs were only cracked and don't bother me anymore."

"I looked over your horse. He'd been shot the way Pecos said, with a bullet in the head. If you hadn't crawled out of that canyon, your death would have been written off as an accident."

"No clues yet, I suppose."

Ed grunted. "Too blamed much snow. No tracks and a flat-nosed slug that likely come from a Winchester .44-.40 rifle. Ain't but fifty men in these parts who carry that."

"Another dry hole." Dave sighed.

"Even the Butcher has holed up from this storm. No one has reported seeing him or having any more attacks."

Absentmindedly, Dave rubbed the old knife wound at his shoulder. "Who could he be, Judge? And why does he want to kill every single woman in the valley?"

"That's a tough question, Bryant. I wish I knew the answer."

"He must be a local man, someone we all know."

"That's the spooky thing about it," Ed muttered. "He might have been in the room with us just minutes ago."

"How many eligible girls in the valley, Judge?" Dave asked.

"Maybe six or seven if you count them from sixteen years and up. Ed and I have spoken to all of them and their families. They are never to be out alone or unprotected. It put a scare into them, but that's better than getting caught by that madman."

"I also slip out and keep an eye on each girl's place for a few minutes each night," Ed reported.

"I ain't had any luck so far, but one day that maniac will slip up and I'll be there to get him."

"Once this snow lets up, maybe we can help you with that vigil," Dave offered. "After all, we were all a long way off when the first victims were killed."

"I'd appreciate the help. I'm wearing myself out, trying to watch every one of them gals at the same time."

"How about the knife? Did you learn anything from it?"

"I showed it around, but no one sees it as any different from a dozen others. I'm afraid there wasn't anything special about it."

"Wish I'd managed to get his hood off," Dave said. "I'm sorry, Ed. I missed my chance."

Ed rubbed his chin thoughtfully. "You took Jake with your fists and then put a slug in Slick Amos. Seems that you would have taken most anyone in a fight."

"He was quick, Ed. I jumped him, but he still stuck me with his knife. I'm for thinking the man is pretty handy."

"We'll get him one day soon," Judge Hammer vowed. "I only hope it's before he kills again."

His hands were numb at his sides, but he huddled against the building without moving. He had stood in the dark until his feet were icy lumps, and his eyes squinted against the wind while a craving gnawed at his insides. The dreams, the torturous dreams had haunted him for weeks. If only the visions would leave him alone. He had suffered until he could stand it no longer. The only release was to strike back.

The light suddenly went out in the house. All was quiet in the frozen world. The five people were asleep, or would be very soon.

The Butcher fumbled to remove his timepiece. He would give them thirty minutes to get fully asleep. Then he would slip into the house and seek out his victim.

It was a crazy scheme. The man of the house was ill, the woman was hard of hearing, but there were three others inside. He would have to find the girl without waking them all.

Even as he stood and stared at his timepiece, he knew that the act he was about to commit was irrational. He was risking everything on the uncontrollable impulse. If the house were awakened, he might have to kill everyone inside.

Unmoving, he did not ponder the sense of the situation. He was primed to kill. The nights of sleepless punishment had beaten down his common sense. He could no longer bear the incredible agony. The only way to combat the torture was to strike back with a vengeance. Only then could he sleep peacefully.

*   *   *

Ed was shaking, not only from the bitter cold but also from an inner mixture of fear and excitement. He had watched the black form against the building for almost an hour, and he kept wondering if it were a man or a dark shadow against the building. Ed had his hand on his gun, his cold fingers laced around the deadly weapon. If only he could hit the man when he moved. He had never been a good shot, but he now needed what skill he had.

The shadow leaned back, then started slowly across the path that led to the Chambers house. The man had a black hood over his head. It had to be the Butcher.

Ed huddled from the cold, but his hand was in his coat. "Hold it right there!" he shouted. At the same time, he stepped out from his hiding place, his gun extended toward the man.

The man did not hold it. He spun toward Ed, jerking something from his coat.

Ed fired at the man, but he knew he had missed. At forty feet he simply couldn't hit his target with accuracy. He pulled the trigger a second time while seeking cover from return fire.

The flash of the other man's gun was instantly accompanied by something slamming into Ed's chest. His legs folded under him and he spilled onto the crust-packed snow.

There was shouting inside the house. The oldest

Chambers boy appeared on the porch with a shotgun. Ed twisted about, searching for the Butcher, but he was no longer in sight.

"What's going on?" the boy cried. "Who's out there?"

"Get Doc Taylor!" Ed gasped. "Hurry up, son!"

Chapter Fifteen

Dave was bundling up for a cold day in the saddle when Pecos came into the house after saddling two horses.

"Rider coming this way, Davy. Looks like Judge Hammer."

Dave frowned. "What could be important enough to get him on a horse in this weather?"

They didn't have to wait long to find out. Hammer entered the house and went directly to the stove. He held his hands close to the fire and sighed with relief.

"Colder than a spinster's heart out there," he said. "How I hate riding a horse when it's cold."

"What brings you out here, Judge?" Dave asked.

163

"I'd sure like a cup of coffee," he replied, looking at Colette.

"I'll warm the pot," she told him. "We finished breakfast a few minutes ago."

He waited until she left the room, then spoke to Dave: "Big Ed was gunned down by the Butcher last night. Ed caught him sneaking into the Chambers place and shot it out."

"Did Ed get him?"

"He figures that he missed him. The Butcher didn't miss his own shot. Ed took a slug in the chest. Doc thinks he'll make it, but he won't be out doing any lawman work for a few weeks."

"Why come all this way to tell us?" Colette had returned with a cup in hand. "There are plenty of people in town for a posse."

Hammer took the coffee and sipped it. "Ah! Nothing like a cup of your delicious brew to warm a man's insides."

"What's on your mind, Judge?" Pecos was impatient.

"I want Dave to pin on a badge until Ed is up and around. We have a fresh set of tracks but no one is willing to tackle the Butcher alone."

"What about a posse?"

"Only a few horses around that can bust trail, Dave. With the cold and a killer running loose, men are afraid to leave their families."

"You say the man left a trail this time?"

"He had no choice. It snowed an inch about dusk last night. With the frozen ice underneath, the tracks ought to be easy to follow. We know where his horse was waiting, but you're the only man able to face up to that killer. There are a number of men willing to ride with you, but not one of them wants the job as a representative of the law."

"My horse is ready. I'll head that way right now."

"I'll pack you some provisions," Colette said, having accepted his decision without argument.

Dave followed her into the bedroom and stood close behind her. He put his hands lightly on her shoulders and allowed her to turn toward him and come into his arms. He held her tightly, knowing that she had to be afraid for him.

"If there's a chance to get that killer, we have to try for it," he said.

"I know," she murmured. "I want to rid the area of him too."

He tipped her head back by lifting her chin with his hand. He kissed her lightly and smiled down at her.

"I'll be back before you know it."

"When?"

"If I lose his tracks, I'll maybe be home for supper. If not, I'll continue until I catch up with him."

"Be sure that you return in one piece," she said

quietly. "I've nursed you back to health from death once. I don't want you getting hurt again."

He kissed her once more and then gathered his belongings for his manhunt. Within minutes Dave and the judge were riding back toward town. It was a sunny day but the temperature was below zero.

"I don't get it," Dave said to the judge. "Do you mean the Butcher was going to enter a house full of people?"

"The man has to be totally mad, Dave. I can't understand how he hides it so well. You'd think someone would get wise to him."

"If I find him, we'll get some answers—right before we stretch his neck in a noose."

Dave sat his horse with several men at his back. He turned and looked hard at Henry Striker. "Someone came in this direction last night. I followed his tracks from town. He gunned down Big Ed. We don't know if he'll make it or not. He said it was the Butcher."

Henry showed total innocence. "I'm telling you, no one came to the house. We didn't see or hear anyone. If that butcher came through, he done it late to mix up his tracks."

"Dead end," Doc Taylor said wearily. "There are tracks of cows and horses all over the yard. We'll never pick out the right trail again."

Dave heaved a great sigh. "So close! We tracked

him this far. If only he had traded mounts or stopped to warm himself in the house.''

''I'm sorry.'' Henry spoke with bitterness. ''I want that dirty son too. He killed my wife. If anyone ought to help put a noose around his neck, I'd sure be the one to do it.''

''Thanks, anyway,'' Doc said. ''Guess we'll head back to town.''

''Me for my own place,'' Dave said. ''I'll be around to see you tomorrow, Doc.''

The six men from town turned toward the trail back to Scofield. Dave took the shortcut that led over the hills to his ranch. However, he rode only as far as the trees. There he stopped and tried to determine his next move.

Henry had said that no one had stopped by the house, but they had men out on patrol to keep the cattle moving. One of them might have seen something. If only Henry would quit fighting him. There was a chance of discovering who the killer was, and that was more important than petty feuding.

Dave made a quick decision and walked his horse back into the familiar little cove. He had seen the Butcher there once before. It was worth waiting a couple of hours to see what transpired at the Striker place. There were no other leads to follow.

Jake listened to Henry's story about Ed's having been shot. He didn't say anything to his pa or Tom, but he felt his heart begin to pound. He had seen a rider the previous night. He had recognized the man and wondered what he was doing so far from his own place. Now it all made sense.

"I'm going up to the east canyon," he announced. "If any cattle are still alive up there, I'll haze them down. The only chance to save any of the herd to keep them out of the brunt of the wind."

"Good idea, son. Me and Tom will get the boys to working what cattle we have left down to the mesa. We cut a lot of ice there yesterday. Maybe the cattle can get some of the grass we uncovered."

Jake picked up his gear and went outside. He checked his rifle loads and then was on his way. The tingle of excitement was in his veins. He was keeping his knowledge to himself, but it was hard to do. This would be his crowning glory. He would no longer have to be ashamed that Dave Bryant had beaten him with his fists. Once he produced the Butcher, he would be hailed as the hero of the entire state.

It was not hard to find the tracks left the night before. It was only a matter of knowing where to look. He picked up the trail and put his horse along the same prints. After two hours he found himself near the Bryant ranch. It was past noon and the snow was falling once more. He almost missed the change of direction in the trail. It caused him to sit and wonder what the Butcher had been thinking.

He can't know I'm behind him, Jake thought. *It's been a few hours since he rode this way.*

Jake studied the faint tracks. The snow was increasing and he might well lose the tracks soon. He had to decide what the man was up to. If he was seeking shelter, there was the new cabin that Bryant had built near the beaver ponds. The herd of Herefords had been moved to the lower canyons for protection from the storm. It was likely that no one was at the cabin.

He eased his mount that way until he spotted the tendril of smoke from the cabin's chimney. The man was there resting up. *I've got him!*

Jake knew that the man was dangerous. To risk sneaking down to the cabin might be to get himself shot. He surveyed the area and figured out the best route for the man to take.

The safest action was to ambush him. He would be hidden back in the trees, ready for the man. It was unlikely that he would stay in the cabin more than a few hours. He would sleep a little and warm up. Once he figured his horse was rested, he would head for home. Jake would sit back and let him ride right into the sights of his rifle.

It was only a few minutes before there was stirring within the cabin. Jake patted himself on the back for his patience. Had he tried to sneak down to the cabin, he might well have been spotted and killed. He warmed his hands while the man saddled his horse. A smile spread across his lips because he would have an easy shot. The Butcher would never know what hit him.

But the man rode out in the wrong direction. He made his way down the canyon, not up to the ridge.

What's he doing? Jake wondered. *Where's he going?*

He gathered up the reins of his horse and swung into the saddle. The bitter cold had let up with the snow, but it was still too much of a chill to hold on to his rifle without numbing his fingers. He put the weapon back into the saddle boot.

Following at a discreet pace, he kept the Butcher in sight. He tried to outthink the man as he rode. It was possible that he was going into town. That would be a nice cover. He could ride in and discover that Big Ed had spoiled the Butcher's shot at another girl. The only other alternative was next to impossible to comprehend.

Soon he learned that the Butcher was not going into town but had turned toward the Bryant house. That was a real puzzle. Did he think he could bum a meal and pass the time of day with Colette, or was he still anxious to kill the woman who had escaped him twice?

Jake decided to close the distance, but from a different direction. He would take the lower trail to the house. With any luck, he would get there at about the same time as the Butcher.

Chapter Sixteen

Colette heard the steps on the snow's crust. She went over to the shuttered window to have a look just as the weight of a man's body hit the door. It cracked the frame and jarred loose the locked bolt.

A scream escaped her lips from the unexpected assault. She was stunned momentarily, then thought of the shotgun. A second blow to the door and it flew off of its hinges. It crashed down between her and the gun, blocking her path.

The intruder had a black hood over his head and a knife in his hand. He leaped into the room and made a grab at her. Colette spun about and raced into the kitchen. She reached for a knife on the table, but the Butcher caught hold of her and knocked it loose.

She screamed in terror, clawed and flailed at the man, and desperately tried to break loose. His grip was like the tightening of a slipknot. He jerked her to her knees, the knife poised high and ready to strike downward.

"Hold it, Braggs!" Jake called from the doorway. "I'll blow you to kingdom come!"

The Butcher pulled up Colette and jumped behind her in a single motion. He was using her as a shield between them. Backing up a step, he put a knife to her throat, ready to kill her.

"Back off!" the Butcher snarled. "Back away or she's dead!"

"Wait!" Jake cried. "Don't do anything dumb!"

Colette froze, her muscles unable to move. She was holding her breath, fearful that she would die in the next second. The Butcher held her with a bruising left arm around her body. The knife was pressed against her throat. She dared not swallow for fear the knife would slice into her windpipe.

"Take a ride, Jake!" the Butcher snarled. "You don't even like this sinful siren. You aren't stupid enough to die for her."

Jake lowered his rifle slowly, then placed it against the wall. "Let's not get excited, Braggs." Then he removed his gun belt and gun, which he dropped onto the floor.

"See that?" he said. "I'm no threat to you. I'm unarmed."

"What's your scheme?"

"We can settle this like men," Jake said scornfully. "You remember what it's like to be a man, don't you, Braggs?"

"You've talked big for your last time, Striker. I could take three like you for breakfast every morning."

"You talk like a real man, Braggs. Let's see if you can back it up."

The grip loosened around Colette and she was suddenly pushed aside roughly. She caught hold of the counter to keep from falling down.

"Get out of here, Sparrow!" Jake shouted. "Get out now!"

Colette didn't have to be told twice. She sprinted across the room and raced out the door. Jake made a grab for his gun at the same time. She didn't see what happened next as she ran out into the snowstorm.

Without a coat, she felt the bitter cold at once. The snow was coming down so hard that she was blanketed in seconds. She blinked back the snow that melted into her eyes. She put her arms across her chest for what warmth she could manage.

The sounds of a scuffle had been extremely brief. When she dared look back toward the house, her heart tried to jump from her chest. The Butcher was hot on her heels.

Dave had been back in the trees, and watched Jake ride past. He was curious that the man kept looking at the ground. It took no real art of deduction to guess that he was following a trail. That could only mean that he knew about the visitor the previous night and was on his tracks.

It was a long journey back toward his own place. His horse was tired from the long hours of bucking the deep, frozen snow, and its legs were raw from the jagged crust of ice. Even so, it managed a pace that kept him at Jake's back and always out of sight.

Dave wondered what was going on when Jake stopped above the line cabin. That just didn't make any sense. After a few minutes Jake was moving again. Within an hour he had led him all the way back to his own house.

From two hundred yards away he had seen Jake hurry to his ranch house. There had been a muffled scream, and suddenly the door seemed to be open or missing. Dave prodded his horse for more speed, but the animal had nothing left to give. Then Colette rushed out of the house and into the storm without a coat. She had not gone fifty feet when another man appeared. Dave recognized the Butcher at once and put his heels to his mount.

Colette fell down in the deep snow and scrambled

ahead on her hands and knees. She was much too slow to escape. Dave's animal was laboring with every step, heaving from exertion. They would never reach her in time. He jerked the animal to a stop and pulled out his rifle. Then he dropped to the ground. He had to be sure.

The Henry was a good rifle and held seventeen rounds. He aligned the sights and, with one eye closed, he held his breath and squeezed the trigger.

The hooded Butcher was right up to Colette. She was crawling in the chest-deep snow, trying desperately to escape. The blast from the gun rocked the stillness of the storm.

Dave fired again and again. Six, seven, eight times. The Butcher was knocked backward into a small tree. It must have supported his weight, because he would not fall.

Dave started forward, still levering round after round into his gun. He fired a dozen times, afraid that the man was invincible. It was not until he drew close enough to see the form clearly that he realized the man was stuck between two branches.

Colette managed to get to her feet, and she waded the deep drifts to his side. She threw her arms around him and clung to him.

"David! Oh, David! He had me!"

"Who is he?"

"Axell Braggs!"

Dave removed his coat and wrapped it around

Colette's shoulders. Then he made his way to the lifeless form. He removed the black hood to reveal the glazed eyes of a dead man. Axell Braggs had been the mad Butcher.

"Jake saved me. He's in the cabin!"

They hurried back to the house. Dave stood the door up and propped it into place while Colette knelt down beside Jake and cradled his head on her lap. When she opened his coat, it revealed the front of his shirt to be soaked with blood.

"Didn't even slow him down," Jake gasped.

Dave examined the man quickly. The wound was a fatal one. He knew that it was only a matter of seconds.

"Why did you risk it, Jake?" Colette asked. "You had no chance."

"Couldn't let him hurt you."

"Me?" she said, incredulous. "Since when did my safety matter to you?"

Jake shut his eyes, his face twisted in pain. "Fooled you all this time, didn't I?"

"What are you talking about?"

He coughed and strained to hold on to life. "I've loved you ever since you moved in with us, Sparrow." He tried to grin, but a grimace replaced it at once. "You got your name changed so I could never take you for my wife. It . . . it ate me up inside."

"But you were so mean to me. I thought you must hate me."

"Had to . . . to do that." He was gasping with each word, fading like the last rays from a sunset. "If you hated me, I knew I could never . . . never have . . . you. . . ." His voice had trailed off to a whisper. Then his eyes turned to glass.

"He's dead," Dave said softly.

"And all the while he made me hate him. He hurt me and punished me all these years and yet he loved me. He was cruel because he could never have me as his wife."

"In the end, he gave his life to save yours," Dave said gently. "I'm real sorry that I misjudged him."

Henry took his boy home. He would be buried in the snow and then given a permanent burial after the frost left the ground. As for Axell Braggs, his foreman took him back to the ranch to lie in wait for proper burial. Men from both ranches packed their gear and left. The herds were lost to the cold and snow, killed off by the thousands.

Pecos and Concho stood by the window while Dave and Colette sat on the couch. Seated on his own chair, Judge Hammer sorted out the details about the mad Butcher.

"The Indians tortured Axell for twenty-four hours. That's a documented fact from the Indian wars. One can only imagine what that kind of agony does to a man."

"He was unable to ever be a real husband to a woman, so he killed them," Pecos said.

"I don't think that it was quite that simple," Hammer commented. "He still had the feelings, the dreams, and the desires, but he could never fulfill his needs. It must have torn him apart inside. It certainly made him a brutal killer."

"How's Big Ed?" Dave asked.

"He's getting better with each passing day. He was shocked to discover that the killer was Braggs, but says that he should have reasoned it out. The man was cunning, a superb fighter with all weapons, and had a history of being tortured by the Indians."

"Tell him that he can have his badge back."

Hammer nodded. "I'll do that."

"Then it's all over," Concho said. "When the weather clears, we'll see just how much this country has been hit by the storm."

A warm Chinook wind blew through the Montana mountains near the end of February. It was too late for Striker cattle, dead to the last cow. Henry, Tom, and Dawson left the valley without a word to anyone. Axell's Box Z had a remainder of less than a hundred head of cattle. Word came from some of the biggest cattle ranches in the country that they had been wiped out.

As for Dave's herd, he lost twenty-six of the hundred, but he still had enough to work with. The calves would each be worth a fortune come selling season.

Pecos stood on the porch with Dave, watching the water form into puddles. Colette came out to hook her arm through Dave's. Dave was enjoying the peace and quiet of the morning sun.

"They's calling this winter the Great Die-up," Pecos said. "Never been a winter kill like this afore."

"Everyone will remember the blizzard of '86 and '87 for years to come," Dave agreed. "There's a lot of rebuilding to do."

"The bank had a mortgage on Axell's place. We can probably buy what few cattle he has left. That'll make us the number-one ranch in the state with only a couple of hundred head."

"Hard to believe," Dave said. "We'll stack feed from here on. If ever another bad winter comes along, we'll be ready."

"Guess I'll mosey up and give Concho and Short Loop a hand. Can't have that wiseacre Concho razing me about being slow and old."

Pecos mounted and rode up the muddy trail to the canyons. Dave wondered if he should go along. There was a lot of work to be done.

"Are you going to stay home today?" Colette asked with a sly smile. "That door never has been fixed properly."

"Maybe you could keep me company while I work."

She leaned over and kissed his cheek. "I'll keep you company, but I don't know how much work you'll get done."

He smiled at her and said, "I'll never refuse such an offer from you. Think I'll spend the whole day fixing the door."